“Your A[illegible] A”

To: David – It's a pleasure to know you
Scott & [illegible]

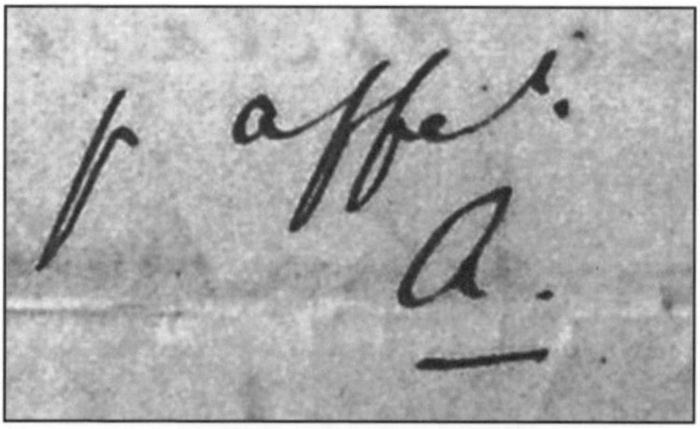

A Collection of

Sir Arthur Sullivan's Letters

to his Family

Selected and edited by
W. Scott Hayes and
Scott M. Hayes

Published in Great Britain by the Sir Arthur Sullivan Society
in June 2015.

ISBN: 978-0-9932993-0-8

Published by the Sir Arthur Sullivan Society
www.sullivansociety.org.uk
Martin Yates
Chairman
chairman@sullivansociety.org.uk

Printed by RCS PLC
Randall Park Way, Retford, Notts. DN22 7WF, United Kingdom.
email: sales@rcs.plc.uk

To Maud Sullivan Lacy – a loving and much loved grandmother

Table of Contents

Introduction

"In the battle of life you want all your strength & all your devotion to each other. Therefore cling to each other with unyielding tenacity & let nothing break the bond." – Sullivan to his nieces and nephews after the death of their mother.

The family bond was extremely important to Arthur Sullivan and nowhere is that importance expressed more eloquently than in his letter-writing. Sullivan was a prolific letter writer, even by the standards of his day. Of his letters to his family, he wrote his mother most frequently, as well as corresponding with his father, brother, sister-in-law, and nieces and nephews.

Much has been written about Sullivan's legacy, especially his music. Sullivan's music rightly reveals his genius. His letters have never been published in any meaningful quantity, and it is in these letters, particularly those to his family, that Sullivan reveals his heart.

While doing some Sullivan research a few years ago, we learned that several hundred of his letters to his family were preserved in the Pierpont Morgan Library in New York City. The Morgan Library kindly gave us access to these letters. We found warmth and humor in them, as well as the importance of family in Sullivan's life. We also were delighted to find wonderful descriptions of events and locations that are not only unusually interesting, but also demonstrate Sullivan's fine writing ability.

We selected the letters to be included in this book on the basis of interest for both the general reader and the Sullivan specialist. We do not claim to have explored all letters Sullivan wrote to his family, but we are reasonably confident we've seen the large majority that are available. Other sources have come from letters handed down through the family. Some of these letters were recently sold in a San Francisco auction to Mr. John Wolfson of New York City.

We hope this book will give the reader a wider perspective of Sullivan the man and writer, and of his closeness and love of his parents, his brother, and his brother's family. Sullivan did not marry so had no immediate family of his own. We, as Sullivan's great-grandnephew and great-great-grandnephew, hope this book of letters is at least a small step in the direction of expressing deep gratitude felt by his extended family, not only for his loyalty to his parents and brother, but also for his great generosity and loyalty toward his brother's family.

Foreword

It was a unique experience to view the original letters. In box after box some of the handwritten letters were single sheets, some folded and written in booklet style, and some written first in one direction, then written directly over the previous writing at right angles to save paper. The originals are fragile, and are enclosed in sheets of plastic within hard covered folders. We digitally photographed each letter. The ability then to re-examine, zoom in, change the contrast, brightness, etc., greatly enhanced our ability to transcribe with accuracy. The letters selected are almost completely presented in their entirety, and only the fewest edits have been made. On the occasion that Sullivan misspells, or even creates an original word, we've left it untouched.

Following the practice of some books of letters, we have included explanatory paragraphs to make clear a sizable passage of time; to define specific names, performances, locations etc., or to admit when we don't know or can't read something. Occasionally another person writes a note within the letter to share with Sullivan's recipient, and we've tried to point out these instances. Much of the information in these paragraphs came from Arthur Jacobs' biography, along with some by other authors, and some from our additional research. Because Sullivan mentions so many individuals, we have also included an appendix of biographical listings for those that are listed multiple times. We have omitted certain well-known individuals – Gilbert, D'Oyly Carte, etc. Since we made the decision to insert explanatory paragraphs, we chose to avoid footnotes and citations, but a full bibliography is listed at the back of the book.

There are a few instances in which we have chosen to omit a sentence or a short passage. A case in point: in one instance Sullivan included a list of persons known to his mother who attended a certain party. When, after research, we realized most of the persons were not in the public eye, we decided to omit the passage. Often we have kept within the letters some names etc. which we were unable to identify.

Chapter One

"He seemed very much satisfied with me."

(Childhood and Musical Training)

The first letter in this collection is written to Sullivan's father, Thomas Sullivan, when Arthur Sullivan was about one month shy of his twelfth birthday. Thomas Sullivan was serving as sergeant bandmaster for the Royal Military College at Sandhurst, while the younger Sullivan was attending a boarding school in Bayswater, about 35 miles from his family. Arthur, who had decided at the age of five to pursue a career as a musician, recounts for his father his introductory meeting and interview with the Reverend Thomas Helmore, then the Master of the Children of the Chapel Royal. Sullivan seems to have taken upon himself the initiative to apply for the Chapel Royal. The chief duty of the boys of the Chapel Royal was to sing at evening & morning services on Sundays at St. James's Palace. Sullivan was chaperoned by his current headmaster, Mr. William Gordon Plees. The letter also refers to Sir George Smart, who had served many years as organist and composer for the Chapel Royal. Sullivan's spelling, punctuation, and word choice is left as written, and it is interesting that Sir George gives an obsolete address for Rev. Helmore.

20 Albert Terrace
April 9th. 1854

My dear Father,

I went to Sir G. Smart yesterday afternoon and took your letter (it was very kind of you to think of me) He is a very funny old gentleman, read your letter, patted me on the head, and told me that I must go to Mr. Helmore at Onslow Square, Brompton. I and Mr. Plees went there and found that he had gone to live in Cheyne Row, Chelsea. When we got there he was not in and would not be back till 7 o'clock p.m. It was then after 6 so Mr. Plees took me into a coffee shop and a cup of coffee and a roll each. Mr. P could not have taken more trouble than he did. It was exceedingly kind of him.

We went back to Mr. H's and found him in. He tried my voice and said it was in very clear [Editor's note: the word "good" is crossed out, and "clear" is written above] order, asked me some of the Catechism, if I had learned anything of Latin, and told me to write my name and when I was born. (bye the bye my age is against me), and took down your address and name. My living out of town is a great inconvenience as though we have 4 or 5 weeks at Christmas, 5 at Midsummer and a few days at Easter and Michaelmas, yet we have always to be there on Sundays. But he has got my name down as a Candidate. He will perhaps send for me sometimes so he has got Mr. Plees address. He seemed very much satisfied with me. He seems a very nice Gentleman.

We got back home again about 8½ p.m. Rather tired. He has not had time to answer Mr. Smith's letter as he has got so many on hand. It was very very kind of Mr. S. to take so much trouble about me. I am very much obliged to him.

Goodbye
God bless you,
your affect. and dutiful
Arthur

Sullivan was accepted as one of ten "Children of the Chapel" just four days later, beginning his musical career on April 12, 1854. He moved into the house that accommodated the Helmore family and all of the boy choristers. The following letter can be dated to Tuesday 13 March 1855, as the statement "something else that will please you" refers to a notice in *The Times* on the previous day announcing a concert of music of the composer Sir Henry Rowley Bishop on Saturday 17 March. The notice reads, in part "For the more efficient execution of many concerted pieces the services of a complete chorus of men's voices will be introduced in this Concert – in addition to the engagements of Masters Sullivan, Cook, Malsch…"

6 Cheyne Walk
Tuesday

My dear Mother,

This is about the 5th time that I have set down to write to you & have continually been interrupted.

Those concerts I spoke of are under the direction of Sir H.R. Bishop. If you look in the first page of Monday's Times you will see the full particulars of it & something else that will please you. I believe I shall get a present for it.

Tell dear Father that Mr. Land is the <u>"accompanyist"</u> (I do not know how to spell it). We have to go to his house to rehearsal at his house. He is a very nice fellow. I told him that it was my father and my cousin that played and sang there, and he was very much surprised at it.

I went there this morning to rehearsal and saw Sir H. Bishop. I cannot write much tonight as I am afraid Mr. Helmore will come down and catch me at it & then I shall get a Wacking, For I ought to be at Latin.

Good night God bless you. Yr. affectionate Son
Arthur Sullivan

I am alright. I shall call for my books soon. Excuse bad writing for I am like the Frogs & Hares. In continual alarms.

As the last letter suggests, Sullivan quickly became one of Helmore's favorite soloists. Helmore was not the only one who noticed Sullivan's talent. Six days prior to the next letter, Sullivan had become the first Mendelssohn Scholar to study at the Royal Academy of Music. The scholarship had been funded in part by Jenny Lind, donating concert proceeds to honor the late composer. Sullivan was the youngest competitor for the scholarship, and as his voice had not yet changed, he continued with the Chapel Royal while studying at the Academy. Sir Frederick Gore Ouseley was a cleric, a baronet and a composer.

Hereford
Saturday Eve.
Sept. 27, 1856

My dearest Mother,

Here we are all safe and sound at the "Green Crayon" for the night – & now I will explain to you how it comes that I am here. Sir Frederick Ouseley has built a church at Tenbury about 25 miles from here and invited Mr. Helmore and four of the boys down to the consecration of it which is to take place on

Michaelmas day next. […] We sleep here tonight, go to the Cathedral tomorrow and go on to Tenbury tomorrow evening, isn't that jolly? We shall come back about Tuesday or Wednesday. Love to all.

Good night.
God bless you.
Your affect. son
A.S. Sullivan

Sullivan threw himself into his studies at the Royal Academy of Music, rubbing shoulders with the best musical talent of the age. Composer and organist for St. Paul's Cathedral, Sir John Goss, served as Sullivan's professor of harmony, and Sir William Sterndale Bennett served as his piano instructor. Sullivan recounts seeing a production of Donizetti's opera *Lucrezia Borgia*, featuring the celebrated singers Giulia Grisi and Giovanni Matteo De Candia, better known as Mario. The Russell family, mentioned here for the first time, will be profiled in greater detail prior to an 1868 letter. Christopher Bridgeman was a fellow chorister. "Helen" probably refers to a cousin staying with Sullivan's parents, and "Fred", Sullivan's elder brother Frederic, is mentioned for the first time.

6 Cheyne Walk
27th. Oct. 1856

My dear Mother,

Having a few moments to spare before prayers, I thought I could not employ it better than writing a line home. I like the Academy very much, but I have a great deal to do. The exercises for Mr. Goss take very near all my spare time. They are very hard – I am to begin counterpoint in a few weeks – won't that be jolly? I am learning one of Clementi's sonatas with Dr. Bennett. It is that one in A. op: 50. It is very nice. I like Dr. Bennett very much indeed. He is so kind. I think I have improved very much.

I saw Fred last Thursday after I came from the Academy. Mr. Russell is going to take us (Christopher) to Drury Lane next Wednesday to hear Grisi and Mario in Lucrezia Borgia. He wrote to Mr. Helmore tonight, and Mr. H. has given us leave, very kind of Mr. Russell isn't it?

The first bell has rung, therefore I must come to a conclusion. Give my love to dear Father & Helen. Has father got his eye on anything yet. Good night dear Mother.

Yr. affectionate son
A.S. Sullivan

P.S. I will write as often as I can.

Sullivan's following review of Anton Rubinstein's performance is interesting, especially since his own future instructor, Ignaz Moscheles, had written about Rubinstein: "In power and execution he is inferior to no one." It should be noted that Moscheles doesn't mention Rubinstein's skill as a composer. Rubinstein played his own Concerto Nº 3, in G, in the first half of the Third Concert of the Philharmonic Society's 1857 Season on Monday 18 May 1857. The conductor was Professor William Sterndale Bennett. In the second half of the same programme, Rubinstein played his own Nocturne in G♭ and Polonaise in E♭. John Ella was a violinist, writer and concert promoter. There is also a reference to composer and conductor Sir Julius Benedict. The mention of "Mrs. Bridgeman" refers to the mother of a fellow chorister, Christopher Bridgeman, referenced in the last letter.

6 Cheyne Walk
May 20th. 1857

My dearest Mother

Having been just doing my double counterpoint, I thought that whilst I had my pen in my hand I would write to you again. While I think of it I want to ask you a few things. Will you rummage up all my old harmony exercises. I know they are somewhere at home, because I shall want them to show at my examination very particularly – The Mendelssohn Committee are going to examine me about the end of this month. I am beginning to look sharp.

I enjoyed the Philharmonic very much last Monday – all except Rubinstein – he has wonderful strength in the wrists, and particularly so in active passages, but there is a deal of clap-trap about him – as for his composition – it was a disgrace to the Philharmonic. I never in the course of my life heard such wretched, nonsensical rubbish before. Not two bars of melody or harmony together throughout, & yet Mr. Ella thinks him wonderful & means to have him at the Musical Union.

I went last night to hear the Liedertafel or vocal association under Benedict. I enjoyed it very much. It is very likely we shall join it. My best clothes are looking dreadfully shabby. I have had them a year. I can hardly wear the trousers. They are so short for me.

Tell Helen she "forked out like a brick" on my birthday, much obliged to her for it. I would have sent the Capriccio long ago only Mr. Goss has not had time to look at it yet. I can't write any more because first dinner bell has just rung. Mrs. Bridgeman is in town. I have seen [her] two or 3 times. She is staying over at Clapham. I introduced Fred to her the other day.

Do not forget please the different things.

Goodbye Dear Mother

A.S. Sullivan (M.S.)
I saw father on Saturday.

In the above letter, Sullivan follows his signature with "M.S." In the following letter, it is clear this stands for "Mendelssohn Scholar." Note the second plaintive mention of shabby clothes. The examination mentioned would determine whether or not Sullivan retained his scholarship for the next year.

129 Tachbrook St.
Saturday 30th. May
1857

My dear Mother,

At the Mendelssohn examination on Thursday, they made me sing one of my songs, and when I had done, Sir George Smart said I was not to sing another note or else I should have no voice at all afterwards because it was breaking. He is going to speak to Mr. Helmore tomorrow about it, so I shall have to leave in a few days. I suppose father wants to know what is to be done about it for this short notice has taken us quite aback as the sailors say. If I should leave next week what am I to do for board, lodging and washing?

Write as soon as you can or perhaps I shall have to go to the Union for relief. Haven't time to write anymore. We bought Helen's music this afternoon. Goodbye. God bless you. My clothes are so small and shabby.

yr. affect. son
A.S. Sullivan
Mendelssohn Scholar
1857 & 1858

Not only was Sullivan granted another year as a Mendelssohn scholar, the honor was extended for a third year, so that Sullivan could study at the Leipzig Conservatory. The recommendation came not only from Sir George Smart, but also Sir Julius Benedict, who had conducted the Liedertafel praised in an earlier letter. We haven't been able to determine the meaning of the "something" mentioned below. However, the letter certainly makes clear how familiar Sullivan had become with the family of Ignaz Moscheles, his piano instructor and mentor. Carl Klingemann served as the secretary for the Academy's Mendelssohn Scholarship committee. Ferdinand David taught both conducting and violin at the Conservatory.

Leipzig 12th. Jan. 1859

My dear Mother,

Sorry to put you to the expenses of another letter, but I have seen Mrs. Moscheles today, & she thinks Mr. Klingemann has something to send to her very particularly. Therefore if it is not troubling Mr. Leiss too much perhaps he would be kind enough to bring it. I am always glad when I can do any little thing for her, as she is so very kind to me. She wants to know if you will be good enough to send round to Mr. Klingemann's to ask. I have nothing to say as I exhausted myself in my last – Last Monday I played the wind instruments of the [Mendelssohn] Italian Symphony from score in the orchestra lesson. David was so pleased that I am to play it again in the Abend-Ünterhaltung when Madame [Clara] Schumann is here next week. Love to all.

yr. affect. son
Arthur S. Sullivan

One year later, Sullivan writes to his father as Thomas Sullivan celebrated his 55th birthday. Sullivan's scholarship had been extended a year, in part due to the continued contributions of Henry Broadwood, the piano manufacturer, allowing the young musician to continue his studies in piano, composition, and conducting. Broadwood also assisted the Sullivan family by employing Thomas Sullivan to oversee a band made up of his factory workers. Now at the end of his second year at the conservatory, Sullivan reports on conducting his own composition. The reader will note Sullivan will soon stop referring to himself by his initials alone, for obvious reasons. Sullivan refers to Konrad Schlemitz, the director of the conservatory. A "Prüfung" is an examination (obviously a concert examination in this case), and a "landpartie" is an outdoor festival. John Barnett is actually John Francis Barnett, nephew of the composer of the same name, the younger being a Royal Academy colleague of Sullivan, who also studied in Leipzig.

Leipzig, 5th. June 1860

That my wishes for you are this day, dear father, I need scarcely repeat to you. You know that I thank God He has spared you for so many years in health, and also that I pray He will continue to do so for many more to come. I can only say a hearty God bless you, and wish I were with you to do it personally.

I enclose you a programme of our last Prüfung. You will doubtless on looking over it recognize one of the names. Translated the thing stands as follows: Overture to T. Moore's poem, "The Feast of Roses", from Lalla Rookh (E major) composed by A.S.S. from London (conducted by the composer). "The Feast of Roses" is the German name for the "Light of the Harem". It was such fun standing up there and conducting that large orchestra! I can fancy Mother saying now, "Bless his little heart! How it must have beaten!" But his little heart did not beat at all. I wasn't the least nervous, only in one part where the drum would come in wrong at the rehearsal in the morning, but he did it all right in the evening. I was called forward three times at the end and was enthusiastically cheered. I shot the bird as Mr. Schlemitz said, i.e. had the greatest success in the whole Prüfung.

The newspapers have also treated me very favourably, much better than I expected, for the Overture being written in Mendelssohn style, and there being such a clique against Mendelssohn, I thought they would have treated me roughly.

I send you some papers with the translations. The "Leipziger Journal" says, "with respect to the compositions, we were gratified at discovering in the youthful Sullivan a talent, which we may venture to say that by the aid of active and continued perseverance gives promise of a favourable future. His Overture was certainly a little spun out, but never the less successful by the aid of well selected materials in mastering the expression of the one definite aim held in view." The "General Anzeiger" says, speaking of the applause which followed Fischer's Quartett, "still more so was obtained by Herr Sullivan in the second part, for his Overture, conducted by himself, which striving toward a new direction transported us into the Persian plains of Moore's lovely poem and gives us great hopes for the young composer." I will send more papers and another letter in a day or two, for I have scarcely any time to write now, but I knew you would be disappointed if you didn't get a line from me on your birthday. We have got another "Landpartie" today and as it is now ¼ past one and they go away at half past, I cannot write much more. I was out all yesterday and today making arrangements, and I am now so tired, I can hardly walk. How are you getting along at Broadwood's? If I write a march will you score it for me for your band there?

Have you seen John Barnett yet? Don't forget the tailor's bill. God bless you again dear Father.
yr. affect son. Arthur

Love to all.

After two years in Leipzig, the Mendelssohn Scholarship could no longer be renewed. Somehow Thomas Sullivan was able to augment his own contribution with other funds to make up the difference, perhaps with contributions from Smart, Broadwood, or even Henry Fothergill Chorley, the music critic who had also been on the scholarship committee. Arthur Sullivan sends his thanks in this letter. Besides Moscheles, he mentions several others who clearly value his tenure – Ferdinand David, John Francis Barnett, and Carl Friedrich Kistner, music publisher. There is also the first mention of Charlotte Louisa Lacy, his brother Fred's fiancée.

Leipzig, Sept. 1860

How shall I thank you sufficiently my dearest Father for the opportunity you have given me of continuing my studies here. I am indeed very grateful and will work very hard in order that you may soon see that all your sacrifices (which I know you make) have not been to no purpose; and I will try to make the end of your days happy and comfortable. I had given up all idea of staying longer and indeed was making preparations for my journey home. Therefore the surprise was greater for me. I had written to Sir George that same week enclosing a letter from Mr. Moscheles urgently begging him to prolong my stay. I am going to leave my present lodging as I find I can live cheaper otherwheres, therefore please address to the Conservatorium 'till you hear from me again. I shall also not live in a family, as having so many acquaintances (Moscheles, David, Barnett, Kistner etc.) where I can go in and sup when I like. I shall of course save so much by it. I shall pay my new lodgings by the month (beforehand). I will let you have a table of my new accounts directly [after] I have moved. I leave here Thursday. Shall you send the money to me or to Mr. Moscheles? Either way, I wish you would write and thank him for the immense trouble and kindness which he has had and shown in taking care of me so long. Also mention Mrs. M's name. He has promised to advance me some money to move with and to pay my first month's expenses. I must now go and secure a room directly, as being fair-time and every place is full I may have some difficulty in finding one.

With best love to Mother, Fred and Charlotte; believe me, dear Father

Your affectionate son
Arthur S. Sullivan

I am in a great hurry, as being Examination time my head is quite bewildered with the number of things I have got to do together with the sudden alteration in my plans.

The detailed musical discussion in the next letter seems evidence of the musical closeness of father and son. Sullivan and his father are apparently having an extended written conversation about the evolving use of instruments. The serpent, a brass instrument had almost completely been replaced by the ophicleide, very popular in Sullivan's day, which in turn was gradually replaced by the mentioned tuba and euphonium. Interestingly, the serpent has become a bit more popular since the 1970s. The contra-fagott is the contrabassoon. Along with Schumann, Sullivan refers to Moritz Nabich, a famed trombonist, as well as composers Friedrich August Kummer, Niels Wilhelm Gade, Victor Cornette, and Friedrich August Belcke – the last two having several compositions with particular elements for brass. He chides against the attitude of the English critics (specifically mentioning his own past benefactor Henry Chorley), and, at least some English musicians, who speak against Schumann. "Zukunftsmusik" translates as "music of the future." Joseph Joachim was an Austro-Hungarian violinist, composer, conductor and teacher. He was a friend of Felix Mendelssohn as well as of both Clara Schumann and Johannes Brahms.

Leipzig November 26th. 1860

My dear Father,

Many thanks for the valuable information regarding the bass instruments which has explained to me everything I wish to know. There is only one point you are mistaken in, however, respecting the word Tuba. If you examine the modern German orchestral scores, you will find it frequently, viz in Schumann, Gade, Wagner, & even so far back as the Choral Symphony of Beethoven. Mendelssohn has it sometimes, but generally employs the Ophicleide. In the "Meeres-Stille" Overture he has written for Serpent & Contra-Fagott. But whatever may be marked in the scores, the part is always played in our Orchestra here by a huge brass instrument, which I think is a Euphonium. But is there no instrument which goes down to G?

I fancy I have seen that note written somewhere.

I am glad to hear you are getting on so well at Broadwood's, for judging from the music you perform, you must have taken immense pains with them. I hope you will let them play the Athalie March to me when I return, as that is a particular favourite of mine, but be careful about the piano in the heavenly Trio as that is so often overlooked. Apropos of your Band. I have looked out a good deal of music for brass instruments. Mr. David wrote a Concertino for Trombone some years ago, which has been played everywhere in Germany & France with immense success. If you remember Nabich made great effect with it last year in London. Mr. D. has lent me his own score to have copied. It is unfortunately with full

Orchestral accompaniments, but he says he heard it once in Prague, performed with military band accompaniments, therefore we are going to try, if we can get them from there, if not you will have to arrange them from the score, which I will send you the first opportunity. It is a splendid piece, not too difficult, & enormously effective. The following pieces may also be useful to you. You can get them at Schott's – Kummer Op:62, and Methode de Trombone par Cornette 2nd part. I have bought some exercises of Belcke's for you, & will send them over by post, as they won't cost much, & will save you a great deal of work perhaps. But you can get a great many of these sort of things at Schott's or Ewer's & even perhaps Augener's. […] I have given up the Symphony. I finished the first movement, but did not like it when it was done for whatever way I turned the second subject, it always sounded like the quintet of Schumann, a piece you do not know of course, being an Englishman. I cannot understand the reason why the critics, & in consequence, musicians themselves, should be so prejudiced against that unfortunate composer; at the very name of Schumann an English musician draws back alarmed, shrugs his shoulders, & mutters a few words about Zukunftsmusik, Weimar, etc. etc. & doubtless with fine judgment, will point out the marked difference between Schumann and Handel! & yet if you ask that man to tell you conscientiously if he ever heard a note of Schumann's music, he will probably be obliged to answer, no--

I am called away suddenly; Joachim & Clara Schumann are going to give a little private matinée in the Conservatorium for the benefit of the masters & students only. After dinner. It was glorious, but Madame Schumann did not play. Joachim played the first violin part, in two pieces, a new Sextett by Mr. David, & also a new Sextett by Brahms, one of the most talented young German composers now living; both very fine works. Madame Schumann is going to play in the Gewandhaus Concert next Thursday. Joachim played a new concerto of his own, and some pieces of Bach, last time, of course wonderfully.

I must close this letter soon as I have a lesson at ½ past two, & must post it on my way. I received both fives that you were kind enough to send me, & am much obliged for them, but do you think it necessary to send me so much, as I draw what I want of Mr. Moscheles, & it only may tempt me to spend more, besides I shall want a little extra at Xmas, there being so many presents to make, & all sorts of little odds & ends that one can't account for. I shall have to draw more than I expected next month, as I have to pay for so many winter things I have had – a new hat, galoshes, new clothes, my great coat, new lined & done up, a comforter, gloves, etc. etc. […] Tell Helen with my love that I thought of her on her birthday, but the day I ought to have visited I was at Moscheles 'till long past posting time, but I will write this or next week.

Love to Mother, Fred, Charlotte, & God bless you, dear Father,

yr. affect. son
Arthur S. Sullivan

P.S. Private. I am writing music to the Tempest!

P.S. Here is a little choice bit. My friend, Wright, happening to be writing to the "Athenaeum" newspaper, also thought he might give a little news respecting the Gewandhaus concerts this year, amongst the things performed was Schumann's music to Lord Byron's "Manfred," which being one of his finest works, & acknowledged as great music by all musicians, was commented upon by him in terms of the highest praise, and in fact lauded Schumann very much. They took the article and printed it with the exception of the whole paragraph about Schumann, which the musical editor (Mr. Chorley, I presume) had cut out! That is a fact from Wright's own lips. Is it not very paltry?

Sullivan's criticism of Chorley did not affect his working relationship, for Chorley wrote the narration for *The Tempest*.

Chapter Two

"I was dreadfully nervous when I first went up on the platform..."

(Early Professional Life)

Four days after presenting selections from his incidental music for *The Tempest*, Sullivan graduated from the Conservatory on April 10th, and wrote to his mother the following day.

Berlin, April 11th. 1861
Hotel Rheinischer Hof

My dear Mother,

I am sorry I have delayed answering your last letter containing the cheque, but what with the Prüfung and the rehearsal beforehand, & packing up & the journey here, I have not had a minute to spare. The "Tempest" was performed in the "Prüfung" last Saturday, & was most successful. I was called forward three times afterwards. I have not seen any papers yet. Madame Klingemann heard from you, I suppose that I was coming to Berlin, and in consequence wrote me a delightful little letter, enclosing one to Mr. P. Mendelssohn which I delivered yesterday, & he has invited me to dine with him today. He is the brother of the Mendelssohn, and is a very rich banker.

[Wagner's] "Tannhauser" is to be given tonight in the Opera house. I shall go & hear it. – I am going back to Leipzig tomorrow (Friday) & shall leave there for England either Saturday or Sunday, so you may expect me either Monday morning or Tuesday morn: about 8 or 9 o'clock – that is certain.

I cannot write any more now for every minute of the day is occupied here in some way or other, besides it will be much pleasanter to tell you everything that has happened here during my stay – Then, au revoir -- this is probably the last letter I shall write you from Germany. Goodbye. God bless you all. It makes me so happy to think I shall see you all again in a day or two.

Arthur S. Sullivan

Sullivan moved back to England from Leipzig to live with his family. Right after the move, he made ends meet by teaching reading, writing and arithmetic for Helmore, and by serving as the organist for St. Michael's Church in Chester Square, London. Several local policemen were members of his choir. His life made a positive turn when he met George Grove, who was later to become the first director of the Royal College of Music, and the founder and editor of the *Dictionary of Music and Musicians*. Grove was at that time employed as the administrator for the Crystal Palace. After hearing *The Tempest* at a party hosted by Henry Chorley, Grove decided to present all of *The Tempest* incidental music at the Crystal Palace on April 5, 1862, and the work was immediately a success.

Sydenham S.E.
October 26, 1862

My dear Mother,

Tonight I dine with Chorley as you know, & it will probably be late before I am home, 12 most likely. How have you been getting on? I have worked like a horse this last week, & have got over a great deal of ground. Mr. Grove and I write on till two every morning, & then have a cigarette & go to bed – I thought to have seen you perhaps on Thursday. I was at the church & gave the police a long grind. The boys sang very much better in tune than they have done for a long time. – I went to dine with Fred & Charlotte last Tuesday & had a very jolly evening. I left at 10, hoping to be home by ½ past, but went to sleep in the train & was carried on to New Cross where I had to stop till 11-20 before I could get a train back home. Very oddly I had boasted in the evening that I could not by any chance go fast asleep in a train, for I always woke at the station!

yr. affect. son,
Arthur

Around the same time, Sullivan was commissioned to write a march to celebrate the wedding of the Prince of Wales. The success of *The Tempest* encouraged Sullivan to write for the opera. He and Chorley began collaborating, and Sullivan approached the conductor, Sir Michael Costa, with a view to working at the Royal Italian Opera at Covent Garden. Through these associations, Sullivan made his first professional appearance as a composer for the stage, with the ballet *L'Ile enchantée,* performed at the Royal Italian Opera House. Costa was also the conductor of the Birmingham Festival, and he commissioned a cantata, *Kenilworth,* from Sullivan and Chorley for performance there in 1864. Sir George Santley, the celebrated baritone, and a leading soprano, Helen Lemmens-Sherrington, were featured. In one mailing, Sullivan writes twice to his father – first, the day before the premiere, then three days following. These fascinating letters end abruptly, as the last page of the second letter is missing.

Birmingham
Wednesday

Dear Father,

I wish so much that I could persuade you to run down tomorrow by the 2:45 train from Euston Square. You could return the same night or I would undertake to find you a bed, somewhere. Bring a little bag with a few dressing things in it & drive straight to 26 Frederic St. Edgbaston where mother is staying. You see 1st. – you will never have another opportunity of hearing the work performed in such a magnificent style again – 2nd. It is a great event in my career & one which I should like you to witness.

Do come (with Fred). There's a dear.

yr. affect. son
Arthur

10 Church Road
Edgbaston
Birmingham
Sept. 11 1864

Dear Father,

I have had no time since Thursday to sit down and write to you, one thing succeeding another so fast – engagement after engagement. However, I know you will like to hear from me that the Cantata was undoubtedly a great success. On Monday night it was rehearsed (I got the first turn, while everyone was fresh) & went extremely well, & people were seemingly much pleased. I had no fear of it not going well on Thursday because the rehearsal inspired me with so much confidence, both in myself & the orchestra. I was dreadfully nervous when I first went up on the platform on the night of the Concert. The Hall was crammed; the fullest evening of the week. Every seat & standing place was filled. I was well received by the audience and the orchestra – and thus encouraged I began.

It went very well indeed, though not quite so well as at the rehearsal. Santley (who sang magnificently) was encored in his song, & Madame Sherrington nearly got one for her and I, but I did not take it, as it was scarcely a legitimate encore.

The pieces which pleased most besides, were the 1st Chorus, the Shakespeare Duet, and the Brisk Dance. I was tremendously applauded, & recalled on to the platform. I have heard a great deal about it since –

After *Kenilworth,* Sullivan began to earn commissions for future work, an overture for the Philharmonic Society of London, and another overture for the Norwich Festival. He was inducted into the Freemasons in 1865, even serving as the fraternal organization's Grand Organist for Queen Victoria's Golden Jubilee. In March of 1866, he premiered his only symphony (later known as the *Irish Symphony*), and in November, his only cello concerto. He wrote several songs and gained status as a conductor. However, all was not golden. Sullivan was having problems completing the Norwich overture, as mentioned in this letter snippet to his father in September 1866:

"I have been at my Norwich Overture all day and the weather has affected the composition, for although I meant it to be bright, it has turned out of a most gloomy and dismal character. It is needless to say that it won't do."

Sullivan's father strongly encouraged his son not to give up on the Overture. Tragically, at the end of the month Thomas Sullivan died, and the as-yet unfinished overture become Sullivan's *Overture in C (In Memoriam)*, commemorating his father's death.

A few months later, through Grove, Sullivan made a connection with the Poet Laureate, Alfred Tennyson, and began exploring the possibility of a collaboration with him on a set of songs. Tennyson was very enthusiastic at first, but as Sullivan's letter suggests, Tennyson was hesitating. The songs were not published until 1871 as *The Window, or The Songs of the Wrens*, and include a tepid preface from Tennyson.

Isle of Wight
10 Feb. 1867

Dear Mum,

As luck had it, directly I got to Symington, it began to rain, and never stopped for the rest of the day. So when I got here, I had a cup of tea and then went and smoked with Tennyson until dinner time. He read me all the songs (12 in number) which are absolutely lovely, but I fear that there will be great difficulty in getting them from him. He thinks they are too slight, & will damage his reputation etc. All this I have been combatting against, whether successfully or not. I shall be able to tell you tomorrow.

It is a little finer now, & we are going for a long walk together to the Needles before dinner. […] Don't come to the station if it is very wet tomorrow.

God bless you.
yr. affect. son
Arthur

Sullivan obviously enjoyed teasing George Grove, whose friendship with Sullivan continued. Sullivan stayed frequently at Grove's home in Sydenham, and this friendship again led to business opportunities. An 1865 biography of Franz Schubert listed a number of works that had never been performed outside Austria, so on behalf of the Crystal Palace, Grove had decided to embark on a manuscript discovery expedition to Vienna. Sullivan was an ideal companion and advisor, for besides their strong friendship, he was fluent in German. The trip was quite successful. They met Carl Anton

Spina, who was responsible for handling all of Schubert's music, who introduced them to Dr. Eduard Schneider, Schubert's nephew.

In this letter Sullivan refers to Chang and Anak – Chang Woo Gow was the tallest man in the world in 1867, and Anak is a giant mentioned in the Biblical book of Numbers. "Jack" is Sullivan's nickname for his brother, Fred.

Vienna
Oct. 9, 1867

My dearest mother,

I should have written to you before, but really it was impossible – the amount of business we have done is quite extraordinary – but the chief difficulty I have felt has been the impossibility of detaching myself from Grove. The charm of that remarkable man is so great, his versatility, his energy, his good looks, his dress, his admirable German (learned in the Strand in 6 lessons – actually 6 lessons) and above all his singular modesty – form a combination as I can safely affirm the world (certainly this world of Vienna) has never been seen. He talks perpetually of you – a theme which you will have no difficulty in believing is the most enchanting possible to me – in short: – but he is looking over my shoulder so I turn to less absorbing topics. […]

We have been at Spina's ever since the early part of the morning, grubbing through manuscripts and making notes, and playing notes and going into ecstasies and sorting out piles until we are nearly dead beat. We didn't leave Spina's until past four then we dined hurriedly. Called at the Poste Restante to see if there were any letters, found none and rushed home to try and get a letter or two written – missed the post, so I left this letter until now (11 o'clock p.m.). I think you left me at Munich last – well, on the Friday morning at 7:40 we left Munich in a snow storm! So we didn't enjoy the (otherwise) beautiful scenery between Munich and Salzburg. We got to Salzburg at 12 o'clock in the middle of the day and there it cleared up a little so as to enable us to get out and about and see the splendid country. It is a wonderfully picturesque old German town surrounded by mountains. We clambered up to the top of an enormous rock where stand the remains of the once famous Archbishop's Palace. It is now partly in ruins and is inhabited by a regiment of soldiers. Right at the summit we went into the Banquetting Hall, the reception and bedrooms, the Torture Chamber (with horrible implements in it) and various other interesting apartments, and certainly had one of the grandest views in Europe. The whole country is magnificent and we could see for miles and miles round, although the weather was not so propitious. Then we went and saw the house Mozart was born and lived in, and the Mozarteum where all relics etc. of him are preserved. Both his harpsichords, various portraits, and many letters and manuscripts are there. When we wrote our names in the visitor's book, the librarian asked me if I was the composer of whom he had often read in the "Signale" and other musical papers. I modestly owned that I did occasionally write a little music, and we bowed and complimented each other. Grove and I left Salzburg the same night and tried to sleep in the train, but for two giants, Chang and Anak, who sat opposite and took up so much room that we couldn't even cross our knees, but sat upright like Egyptian statues. However, we got to Vienna at ½ past 9 the next morning, without much serious damage to our constitutions, and enjoy ourselves now so much that we shall be dreadfully sorry to leave the place, and feel as if we had been here a month.

We have had an enormous success with our work. Mr. Spina has behaved quite nobly to us – anything kinder it would be impossible to conceive. He gave up his rooms to us today, with all the manuscripts carefully arranged, plenty of cigars on the table, and pens, ink and paper and nothing to disturb us. We selected a heap of things and he is going to have them at once copied and sent after us to keep for ourselves and to perform them when and where we like, only of course not to print them. He gave us a strong letter of introduction to Dr. Schneider (a relation of Schubert's) from whom we succeeded in getting two symphonies and an overture! O joy!

We have called upon two or three of the principal musicians here (Esser, Pohl, Hellmesberger etc.) all of whom we have enchanted by our pleasant and fascinating manners. We went on Sunday afternoon over to the burial ground where Beethoven and Schubert lie. We stood a long time at their graves and got some ivy off each.

Tonight we have been talking to an old clerk in Spina's shop who knew Beethoven, Schubert, Czerny and all these fellows well. He told us lots of interesting things all of which we note down in books we carry about with us especially for that purpose. We look like a couple of Mr. Pickwicks.

I think we shall leave here on Friday (if we can finish off our work tomorrow) at 1:30, and get to Prague (where Grove intends to visit the scene of the celebrated battle with a pianoforte, and bring home a few cries of the wounded for the Saturday Concerts). The same night we shall look about us a little and go on to Dresden sometime Saturday, and shall get to Leipzig, which is only three hours from Dresden, Sunday night or Monday. Mind I expect a letter awaiting my arrival there, addressed to the Conservatorium. I have had such nice letters from Moscheles, Reinecke and Schleinitz and have sent them my scores yesterday.

I hope Jack received my "little birdie" safely. I shall leave this open until after I have been to the Poste Restante tomorrow. [...] Good night. God bless you.

Thursday. We have been at work all day and have unearthed two things we have been looking for for four years! No letters, no news. We must copy music all tonight.

yr. affec.
A.

The "two things" to which Sullivan refers are the manuscript discoveries of two Schubert symphonies – the "Tragic Symphony" and another in C major. After leaving Vienna, Sullivan stopped in Leipzig, where he was able to conduct his *In Memoriam* overture as part of the Gewandhaus orchestra series. Grove also leaves a message for Sullivan's mother at the end of the letter.

Leipzig 18 Oct. 1867

Dearest Mum,

You will like to know about the Overture. It was a great success. I went on to the orchestra, undaunted by the frigid audience, made my bow and began. It went splendidly – with great delicacy and great fire. I expected applause, but I got more – a hearty recall after I had left the orchestra.

Everyone of note came and congratulated me afterwards, and I really think it has laid a firm foundation to a good reputation in Germany. Kistner I believe is going to print the Overture.

Next Monday the Symphony is to be tried, and then I leave for Paris. Grove arrived yesterday and is again happy as the separation was telling on his health+. He sends his love. So do I.

yr.
A.
+Bosh! Yours affectionately
G. Grove

Sullivan's professional and personal life continued on quick trajectories following his return from the Schubert expedition. Sullivan created his first operetta, *Cox and Box,* with Francis Burnand, a writer (and later editor) for *Punch. Cox and Box* was first performed for a private party in 1866, and had its first public performance in 1867 as part of a benefit for the widow and family of *Punch* artist Charles Bennett. During this same period, when Sullivan would occasionally stay in Sydenham with

Grove, he grew to know Grove's neighbors, the John Scott Russell family. He became romantically involved with the second of three daughters, Rachel. Her parents were not particularly pleased, and the relationship continued in secret. Rachel and Sullivan were allowed to see each other when the family visited Switzerland. It should be noted that Sullivan had also begun a secret romantic relationship with the third Scott Russell daughter, Louise. It is during this trip that Sullivan wrote to his mother on the second anniversary of his father's death – the "dear one" in this letter. "Uncle and Aunt" must refer to Sullivan's father's brother and sister-in-law, John and Jane Sullivan. "Amy" was Sullivan's eldest niece, about five years old at the time of the letter.

Hauser Frères
Schweizerhof
Lucerne
Sunday
20 Sept. 1868

Dearest Mum,

I wake up here this morning and just in front of my open window is the great mountain Pilatus looking so majestic and beautiful in the morning sunshine. It is too lovely for description. We left Zurich last night and came here to sleep. We are joining a little tour into the mountains returning to Zurich on Tuesday. The Bishop of London and Mr. Tait are here and I had a long chat with them last night after the table d'hote, and introduced Mr. Scott Russell to them. I have now only ten minutes to write in, as the boat goes at 9:20 down to Alpnach, our next pied a terre – but I want you to have this on Tuesday, so that we may all be together in spirit. I shall be spending Monday peacefully and happily in the mountains, which is what I shall like best. I know you have thought me hard and perhaps unfeeling sometimes dear Mum, but I could never trust myself to speak of the dear one. I got always so sick and "chokey", and it was no good scolding you if I myself were to show weakness. Now I am much stronger and can talk and think of him quite calmly and peacefully, and like to do so.

I got your letter at the Poste Restante, and was glad to hear you were well and happy. Give my love to Uncle and Aunt and all of them. Kiss Amy for me, and tell her to be a good girl and pray for her dear Grandpapa.

God bless you dear
yr.
Arthur

Chapter Three

"I have been slaving at this work and hope it will be a success."

(Continued Professional Success; First Partnership with W.S. Gilbert)

There is a significant gap in this letter collection, and a quick biographical narrative is needed. The relationships with both Rachel and Louise ended by 1869. Sullivan started a relationship with American Mary Frances (Fanny) Ronalds, who had separated from her husband two years earlier. The relationship was at first casual and social, and then grew more intense when Fanny moved to London in 1871. Fanny had a beautiful alto singing voice. Sullivan felt that she sang his *The Lost Chord* more beautifully than anyone.

***Cox and Box* had garnered positive attention from W. S. Gilbert in *Fun* magazine, and Sullivan and Burnand teamed up again to write the opera *The Contrabandista* in 1867, but their success was not repeated. Sullivan was more successful with his other efforts, writing seven part songs in 1868, the short oratorio *The Prodigal Son* in 1869, and the *Overture di Ballo*, in 1870. In 1871, the Tennyson song cycle was published, Sullivan composed incidental music for a production of *The Merchant of Venice,* as well as his most famous hymn, *Onward, Christian Soldiers.* For the 1871 Christmas season, Sullivan collaborated for the first time with W. S. Gilbert, creating the operetta *Thespis*, which closed on March 8th of the following year. Sullivan continued to write in several genres – in addition to writing hymns published by the Society for Promoting Christian Knowledge (SPCK), his *Festival Te Deum* celebrated the recovery of the Prince of Wales from typhoid fever in 1872, his oratorio, *The Light of the World* premiered in 1873, and he wrote incidental music for a production of *The Merry Wives of Windsor* in 1874. The choral rehearsal Sullivan mentions is for *The Light of the World.* The rumors Sullivan mentions about knighthood were indeed premature – Sullivan wasn't knighted until 1883. "The Hornet" refers to a satirical magazine. Three years prior, the magazine published a cartoon of Charles Darwin as a "Venerable Orang-Outang", with the subtitle, "A Contribution to Unnatural History".**

The Elms
Eccles
Nr. Manchester
Wednesday
25 Feb. 1874

Dearest Mum,

If you are bothered again by newspaper reporters, just say that so far as I am concerned I know nothing about the proposed knighthood beyond what I have seen in the newspapers. I don't see why I should be "interviewed" on everything that may be said about me. There is of course no foundation for such a thing, and only grows out of the good natured fancy of the "Hornet".

I had a splendid choral rehearsal last night. The chorus is very fine – good tone and splendid attack. It all bids fair for tomorrow's performance. There is to be a crammed house, I am told, and everyone is very keen about it.

This morning I was up at ¼ to 8! I didn't like it though, and am rather sleepy now. I have been writing hard, copying (for Santley and others) the new bits in the Oratorio, correcting a batch of proofs from the S.P.C.K. which arrived here by post, and composing a hymn tune. [...]

Goodbye. God bless you. Love to all.

yr. affect.
A.

Sullivan, while visiting the Earl of Shrewsbury at Alton Towers, writes a letter of condolence to his mother regarding the death of her brother, Arthur Joseph Coghlan. Lord Shrewsbury was president of the Birmingham Festival. John Boosey was the owner of Boosey and Sons, publisher of some of Sullivan's music, and also produced the highly popular Boosey Ballad Concerts.

Stafford
31st March 1874

Dearest Mum,

I was much grieved to hear of poor old uncle's death although I expected it, & thought of him last night a good deal – and I know how much you will feel the snapping of the "last link" as you justly say. Poor old boy, he had a hard and difficult struggle through life, & it seems incomprehensible why he should not have had some sort of reward for it in this world. I am glad you sent them the money. I will give anything you want for the same purpose.

I shan't come home tomorrow not until Thursday. This will give you time to have things put straight again. The biscuits had not come this morning – perhaps they have now, but I have only just come back from Alton Towers where we have been since the early morning. What a lovely place it is! Lady Shrewsbury took me all over house, grounds & everything. She is so kind to me.

God bless you
yr. affect.
A.

Tell Fred to get from Boosey what he wants

Mr. and Mrs. David Beach Grant were long-time American friends of Sullivan. They requested that Sullivan help Mrs. Grant by accompanying her and her large entourage at least part way toward her destination, a "Spa" in Kissingen, Germany. As it happened, she truly needed the help. The next two letters deal with this trip, and were written when he was thirty-three, the same year as he wrote *Trial by Jury*. The letters are good examples of Sullivan's thoughtfulness, kindness, and willingness to go the "extra mile" for others. Sullivan developed a friendship with the brothers Alfred and Leopold Rothschild, who were members of the wealthy, philanthropic Jewish family. Mayence is the French word for the city of Mainz. Jack refers not to Sullivan's brother, but to a servant.

Hotel Disch
Cologne
Sunday, 1875

Dearest Mum,

No need to say I arrived safely because you see it. But I arrived tired – that you may not know. It was an uncomfortable journey, and nothing but the fact that I don't think my friends could have got on without me would have made up for the inconvenience of my extra route. In the first place, I had 5 others in a stuffy, smoking carriage to Dover and could hardly move. And then we had a crossing which knocked everybody's inside out. It was a beastly, chopping sea, and everyone was ill except myself, nearly. I lay down near the centre as usual and dared not move. Once I raised myself to speak to the steward, but I quickly resumed my position, otherwise it would have been all up with me. At Calais a compartment, thanks to Alfred Rothschild, had been kept for us, and we all, servants and children, bundled into it and opened the lunch basket, ate and drank, and enjoyed ourselves to Brussels

But there our luxury ceased. We were hurried from one train into another (that is where I lost Jack) and had a vexatious and tiresome journey onto here where we arrived a little before 12. When I bring you over, we will come by easier stages. The result is that poor Mrs. Grant is utterly knocked up, and is only getting up now (3 o'clock). I have been out with the children. We went into the cathedral and heard a pretty children's service. It is a blazing hot day, the first they have had here, and the cathedral was so peaceful and cool it did one good and took us out of this world for a time. When the service began, the organ struck up, and then in the far distance the boys' voices were heard singing a little motet, and they came nearer and nearer singing all the while. The result was I burst out crying, as I always do at children's voices. I have no doubt the music was weak, and the boys' voices execrable, but the whole thing moved me and did me good. The priest, after the service, which was a sort of little litany, gave a short address. It seemed earnest and simple, but as my young folks didn't understand a word, I brought them out.

Now we are going to dine. I don't know quite what to do. Mrs. Grant is so ill, and the maids are so helpless that I hardly like to trust them alone. Tomorrow morning at nine we all leave – they for Kissingen, I for Paris. Fortunately we go as far as Frankfurt together, which is a good step on the way. I will write again on Tuesday, and let you know my doings

God bless you. […]
yr. affec.
A.

Hotel de Russie
Kissingen
21st. July, 1875

Dearest Mum,

After I wrote to you from Cologne there came the most tremendous thunder storm I have seen for years; lightning terrible to see, cracking claps of thunder and rain like a water spout. And they said in town that they had had many like it lately. Well, it had the effect of making everyone frightened and ill, and turned our insides out. The next morning it was fine and sunshiny, and off we started at 9 o'clock; but poor Mrs. Grant was so weak and ill that she could hardly move. Still, I thought, this fine day, and pretty scenery might do her good; and she and I and the two children got a nice compartment to ourselves so that we were fairly comfortable. But instead of getting better, she fainted dead off and terrified the life out of me for Marie was in the next compartment with the nurse and baby, and the children were of no use to me. Fortunately I had got a bottle of Eau de Cologne in my bag, and I bathed her with that and revived her, but when we got to Mayence (where I should have left her and gone to Paris) she seemed so helpless and wretched that if it had cost me a month's time and a hundred pounds I would not have let her go on alone. And so to get out, change my ticket and get my luggage out of the luggage master's hands (my luggage was registered to Paris) was the work of a very short time. And when I told her I was going to accompany her, it was worth a year of one's life to see her gratitude, dear soul.

The journey here was easy enough for me, but it would have been nearly impossible for them for we had to change carriages and platforms four times, and not one of them speak a word of German, and no guard on the line speaks French! It was touching, but ridiculous to see that once happy family huddled up miserably on the platform, the mother propped against a post, and the baby making eyes and gestures at all the men who passed her, and two maids looking miserable and wronged. But, after all, I brought them all (every box and bag and umbrella too!) safely and triumphantly to Kissingen, and we made a fairly effective entry. The only drawback was that I had telegraphed for Mrs. Grant's rooms, and when I arrived there was no room for me. The hotel was crammed. At last they provided me with a luxurious apartment some few steps above the roof (as far as I could make out) and I managed to settle down and get a little sleep. The next day our poor friend couldn't move; and so I had to bustle about and get good apartments, a tutor for Douglas, hire a pianoforte, and a thousand other little things, besides having the care of the children. I got some very nice rooms, fairly reasonable, and today Mrs. Grant has moved into them, and is very much better and stronger, and begins the "Cure" tomorrow. Now that she is well, and I have seen them comfortably settled, I can go away with an easy conscience, and accordingly at 8:10 tomorrow morning (!) I leave for Paris. I should very much like to stay longer here for it is lovely weather, and is a queer, pretty place. And so tomorrow I go. I will write again from Paris, but I hope to be home on Monday. God bless you.

yr. affect.
A.

Sullivan renewed both private and professional acquaintance in Paris. "Galignani's" was the first English bookshop established on the continent. Christine Nilsson was the famous Swedish operatic soprano. Sir Coutts Lindsay, and his wife, Lady Lindsay were friends of Sullivan. Lady Lindsay's mother was born a Rothschild. Sir Coutts had been a Grenadier Guards officer, and later devoted his time to the arts. T.W. Robertson was a playwright who directed his own plays. Gilbert actually credits Robertson for teaching him how to manage the staging of plays.

Grand Hotel, Paris
Friday, 23 July, 1875

Dearest Mum,

The above is where I live, but I am writing this at Galignani's Library. I left Kissingen at 8 o'clock yesterday morning and travelled straight through to here where I arrived at 11 this morning! Not bad for one journey was it? However, I slept pretty well in the train between Strasbourg and Paris, and when I got here I had a good bath and toilet. Called at Arthur's and found your three letters, and then had a good breakfast. […] I left dear Mrs. Grant very much better – comfortably settled in her lodgings – everything arranged for her – very grieved to part from me, and very grateful for what I had done for her. I didn't see her in the morning before I left, but I called and impressed the landlady with the necessity of taking care of her, and of giving them all lots of clean linen – sheets, towels etc.!

There was an English lady and gentleman in the carriage with me. After a time we got into conversation, and soon exchanged cards. "What, are you Arthur Sullivan?" said the lady. "Well this is delightful". He was a rich, retired clergyman named Chapman, and pressed me to go and stay with them in the country. They left me at Heidelberg (3:30), and I took the rest of the journey alone without any particular interesting incident. He promised me to write to the English clergyman at Kissingen whom he knew very well to ask him to call upon Mrs. Grant.

I telegraphed to you from Würzburg as I thought you might be uneasy at not hearing from me. I see there is nothing in your letters requiring any effort on my part, as you have done everything wisely for me. I don't think I can leave here before Monday, as I promised Robertson to wait for him here, if possible, and he arrives tomorrow he tells me. Mr. Chapman, my travelling friend, told me there was something in the *Times* about my being overworked.

I wish you would send up to Nilsson tomorrow morning, and tell her I am in Paris and anxious to know if I can do anything for her before I return. If you write tomorrow, or she writes, you must address to the Grand Hotel, as Arthur's doesn't open on Sunday. God bless you.
yr. affec.
A.

Write a note to Lady Lindsay and say I am in Paris and shall be home Monday or Tuesday. She is in town.

Sullivan writes to his eldest niece, Amy, in his typical mock-moral style. Edith and Florry (Florence) were Amy's younger sisters.

Hotel Vendôme
Place Vendôme
Paris
29 Sept. 1875

My dear Amy,

This is goose day, and it is very well named from the number of geese whom I have had to see me this morning. The packet of letters you posted arrived all right, but as I changed my hotel to please some friends, I did not get it until later in the day. I am very glad you like your school & I hope you will not waste a minute of your working time in playing, nor waste a moment of your play time by working. That's the way to be thoroughly happy. Be warned by the dreadful example of your unfortunate uncle who did not get up 'till ten o'clock this morning and did not want to get up then, but Adele is so cruel to us in the morning she will not allow me any peace. She comes into my room, & sits on my bed, & then makes a dreadful fuss, so that I am obliged to get up. You remember Adele don't you, Mrs. Grant's child?

Now goodbye, for I have got a heap of letters to write. 6 French, 2 German, & 1 Italian! What do you think of that? A Dutchman also writes to me in his native musical tongue, but although I understand it, I can't write it, so I shall fire off a shot in English to him, in the hope that he won't understand it, & therefore won't bother me again. Much love to Florry & Edith.

yr. affec. uncle

Arthur Sullivan

Sullivan accepted the conductor responsibilities of the Glasgow Choral and Orchestral Union. Six concerts were planned. The first was held on November 16, 1875 in the Glasgow City Hall. Sullivan's childhood mentor, the Rev. Thomas Helmore had been visiting Sullivan's brother, Fred. Based on the subsequent letter, we assume Fred was ill.

144 Holland Street
Glasgow
Sunday

Dearest Mum,

Here's my engagement list for this week.

Monday – Rehearsal
Tuesday – Rehearsal & Concert. Glasgow
Wednesday – Rehearsal & Concert. Greenock
Thursday – Rehearsal & Concert. Perth
(start at 9 in the morning & sleep there)
Friday – Rehearsal & Concert. Dundee (sleep there)
Saturday – return to Glasgow. Rehearsal at 2.
Concert at 7

That's pretty well, with traveling.
I am dead tired today. Next week I shall be knocked up I fear, if it is bad weather. It has been horrible all this last week. Thick fog & heavy rain alternately. But we do our work valiantly & the Band & myself work well together & are covering ourselves with glory – but not money. Apropos of money – the enclosed is pocket money – as you desire, I send expenses straight to Charlotte.

I am glad Mr. Helmore has been to see Fred. He is good in every sense. A thoroughly good, religious man, & a kindly man of the world as well. There's a wretched creature on the floor above me who plays the piano a little. He or she has been playing my hymn tunes all this afternoon. I hope they don't do it out of compliment to me, for they put their own harmony, which to say the least isn't as good as mine.

God bless you,
yr. affec.
A.

On January 18, 1877, Sullivan's brother, Frederic, died of tuberculosis at the age of 39. His widow, Charlotte, was left alone with her large family of children, the oldest being only 13. Sullivan immediately took over the position of guardian and provider. His guardianship included all eight of his nieces and nephews – Amy, Florence, Edith (who died a few months after the death of her father), Herbert (Bertie), Maud (the editors' grandmother, and great grandmother respectively), Frederic Richard (Dickie), and George. At the time of Frederic's death, Charlotte, was pregnant with an eighth child, named William. Sullivan took particular responsibility for his eldest nephew, Herbert (Bertie). Bertie lived with Sullivan as his son, though never formally adopted. Bertie was sent by Sullivan to Brighton to study with a tutor.

Sept. 9 1877

Dearest Mum,

I was up with the whiting and the lark this morning and in town at 11. I have had a tooth stopped, and been under the hands of the surgeon. I have had several business interviews also.

Now to business. I have arranged for Bertie to go to Brighton at once. I settled everything yesterday, and I like the people he is to go to very much. Mrs. Kuke recommended them – has known them for years, and says they have done wonders with boys. Mr. Marmery is a master in the College, but Bertie will be chiefly in the hands of Mrs. Marmery, who teaches her own children herself every morning for three hours. I liked her very much. I will take Bertie down tomorrow (Sunday) by the 5.50 train from Victoria.

I should like you and Charlotte to have the carriage and drive up here when you have finished dinner, and bring his clothes and books. We can have tea here, and then I will tell you more details – you can be here between 3 and 4. I have to see my doctor again at 2. […]

God bless you
yr. affect.
A.

The opera referred to in the next letter is Gilbert and Sullivan's *The Sorcerer*. Jane ("Janie") Sullivan was Sullivan's first cousin, the daughter of Sullivan's father's brother, John.

9 Albert Mansions
Thursday night
Nov. 1, 1877

Dearest Mum,

I am just putting the last few bars to my opera, and tomorrow begin the scoring, so it is a favourable occasion to write a line to wish you many happy years to come, and that I hope and pray God may bless and keep you. Janie Sullivan told me at rehearsal this morning that she had seen you going to the oratory, and that you looked so well and nice, and that pleased me.

I have been slaving at this work and hope it will be a success. Everything at present promises very well. The book is brilliant and the music I think very pretty and good. All the company are good, and like it very much.

The scoring will be a tremendous labour, but I don't mind that, as I can do it quickly, and there is no more composition to be done. […]

God bless you
yr. affec.
A.

The Exhibition Commission referred to an international exhibition held in Paris. Sullivan's involvement must have been to discuss the British contribution. Sullivan tells of his mourning for his brother, Frederic. Silva was Sullivan's servant. Charles-Marie Widor is the full name of the resident organist at the Church of St. Sulpice in Paris. The phrase "I hope I shall come back strong and well" refers to Sullivan's violent kidney disease attacks through much of 1877.

Hotel Vendôme, Place Vendôme
Paris Christmas Day 1877

Dearest Mum,

It is very wet and miserable looking outside, but my fire and café au lait tend to give an artificial cheerfulness to my rooms – so before I go out to see the President of the Exhibition Commission I write a few lines of a contented nature. The Dramatic profession of London have mustered in great force here for Christmas. I meet someone I know, from Carte to David James, at every turning. Of course they all go back today for their Boxing Day performances, and a nice crossing they will have – if it is anything like the one I had. I had a cabin and lay down, so kept my balance all the way, but those who were not so fortunate had a bad time of it. Silva looked green and yellow when we arrived at Boulogne. "Ah monsieur, quelle traversée epouvantable!" said he. I swaggered and said I hadn't noticed it, but I was deuced uncomfortable all the way.

Last night I went to midnight Mass at St. Sulpice where my friend Widor is organist. The crowd at the door was like the gallery of a theatre on Boxing Night, and I had to fight my way through – nearly crushed to death. However by the help of a stalwart gendarme I got in at last, and then went up to the Organ Loft where I found Widor, Mad[ame] Trélart, and one or two other people I knew slightly. When the mass was over, that is the communion, judge my surprise and pleasure when they struck up the Adeste Fideles! The harmonies they used disturbed me a little, but on the whole I was very glad.

At all the churches the crowd was enormous. I think I shall stay here tonight and go off to Nice tomorrow, as it is wet and cold. I shall have a quiet dinner with the Parsons who are as anxious as I could be not to dine entirely en famille. I have gone out of mourning for today, and shall put it on again tomorrow till the end of the year. But I don't see why I should wear black on dear old Fred's birthday. So I brighten up, and shall drink a glass of wine to his memory, bless him, just as I should to his health if he were alive. He would have done the same for me I know.

It is of no use grieving and repining. Those who are left have cares and responsibilities, and must brace themselves up and face them courageously. I hope I shall come back strong and well, for I have much to do this forthcoming year. Now goodbye and God bless you. I am with you all in my thoughts. I hope the children liked their little presents and that they will spend Christmas happily.

yr. affec.
A.

Bertie had written to Sullivan from his boarding school. It doesn't appear that his school would be proud of his spelling skills. Juliette Conneau, an excellent amateur singer, was married to the physician of Napoleon III. She put on a concert for Sullivan on February 18, 1878 in Nice. At this concert, Sullivan conducted the *Merchant of Venice* music, the 'Graceful Dance' from *Henry VIII* and the *Overture di Ballo*.

Monday, 11 Feb. 1878
Nice

Dearest Mum,

I thought I had a letter from you on Saturday, but when I opened it I found it was from Bertie – and a very good letter too. He tells me various items of news. Amongst others, that at football he got three "keeks" on the leg, and that he tried to "brake a piece of lickerish, and just done it". He seems jolly enough.

I have been fully occupied since I last wrote in preparing for Mad[ame] Conneau's concert which is to take place this day next week and of course the orchestral arrangements give a great deal of trouble. We are so far advanced that the first rehearsal takes place this evening. I shall then be able to see what the band is like. I expect it will require a good deal of working at. The bills and posters are out all over the town, and my name is a good deal discussed. I am only writing a few lines now just to show I'm alive, and will write fully tomorrow and tell you all about the rehearsal and other things.

Give my love to Charlotte. Tell her I was glad to get such a nice letter from her. God bless you.

yr. affec.
A.

Illness was unfortunately an almost lifelong experience for Sullivan. The following letter gives an example of his dedication to music regardless of illness. Markham Law was an assistant to Sullivan.

Monday 18 Feb. 1878

Dearest Mum,

I daresay you were getting anxious at not hearing from me, and so I polished off a telegram this morning early to let you know I was all right. Last Tuesday morning I had my second rehearsal of the band at the theatre. It was a beautiful sunshiny day, but the theatre was cold, and as it afterwards transpired, I sat in a thorough draught all the time. Directly after my déjeuner I felt ill and headachy and feverish, and so went home to bed, from whence I did not get up again until Sunday. I had two doctors, and I told them that whatever was the matter with me I <u>must</u> be well enough to go out on Sunday for the last rehearsal of Mad[ame] Conneau's Concert. So I passed through a violent crisis – racking rheumatic pains all over me – my head like a furnace, and my throat closed up so that I could only swallow a little liquid, and that with great pain. Somehow, I pulled through and got better, and yesterday saw me at my rehearsal – weak but able to do the work. Today I am as right as possible and feel all the better for my clearing out. During my illness, dear Mad[ame] Conneau was as good as gold – just like a mother. She brought me a warm flannel dressing gown of her own for me to sleep in, came always three or four times every day to sit with me and see if I wanted anything, and was dreadfully concerned altogether. Markham Law came in one day, on his way home from Italy, but I would not let him or anyone write to you in case it might frighten you, and make you believe I was worse than I really was. Of course had there been any danger you would have known instantly, as I was surrounded by people who cared for me and knew me. Today is the great Concert, and here is 12 o'clock, and I must go and arrange the orchestra. So no more today. I will write when it is over and tell you all about it.

Don't write here anymore, as I shall probably leave Thursday or Friday en route for England.

Love to Charlotte. God bless you.

yr. affec.
A.

Prince Alfred, Duke of Edinburgh (1844-1900) became a close friend of Sullivan. Sullivan became the principal of the National Training School for Music in 1876, occupying the post for five years. The concerts referred to are in all probability the Promenade Concerts in Covent Garden held during the summer of 1878. Sullivan was the conductor. "Old Jimmy" was James W. Davison, a music critic and friend who was a strong supporter of Sullivan's music. Ambroise Thomas was the celebrated French composer, and pianist Caroline Montigny-Rémaury was Thomas' sister-in-law. "Flys" were carriages for hire.

9 Albert Mansions
S.W.
Monday

Dearest Mum,

I have just written a long letter to the Duke of Edinburgh and thanked him for his kindness to the children, and told him all about the School of Music.

I had a few lines from Charlotte this morning just saying that they had been to the Palace and that the Duke and Duchess had been very kind to them. I enclose one I had also from Mrs. Bourne and it will please you. What a dear, kind affectionate soul she is. You might write to her. Are there flys at Newbury Station?

Because if it is a fine day on Thursday, and I can get off rehearsal, I should like to run down and see you by the 9 o'clock train from Paddington returning by the 5.15 in time for the concert. Then I will bring some salmon and a piece of green paper with me unless you want the latter sooner. A magnificent article in the *Times* today again. Old Jimmy is a trump. He comes regularly to the Theatre every evening. What a miserable day yesterday was. I stayed in 'till 6 o'clock, then went and called upon Mad[ame] Montigny (our pianist, who has gone back to Paris today) and took her out to dinner. She is a great friend of Mad[ame] Conneau's and I dined at her house when I was in Paris to meet Ambroise Thomas. I came home early and went to bed, but it was so stifling hot I could not sleep.

How far are you from Reading to drive?

God bless you
yr. affect.
A.

Sullivan mentions a recurrence of his painful kidney problem. Hock is German white wine. Friedrickshalle water is a kind of mineral water, imported from Saxe-Meiningen for the treatment of digestive disorders. Sullivan was probably writing *H.M.S. Pinafore.*

9 Albert Mansions
Wednesday

Dearest Mum,

If you are ordered the hock of course I will send some, but I should have thought it a little too heating for the gout. I have been very bad all day, with my liver in such great pain that I had to go and see my doctor. It is the incessant writing and sedentary work. Thank God another fortnight will see it finished, then a drive and dinner at the Orleans now and then will do us good. I am in great pain now, but the medicine will probably relieve that shortly. I forgot to send you the Friedrickshalle water but I daresay you can get that at Fulham. Is Charlotte better? I hope so – it is very bad for us all to be ill at the same time. You looked much better on Sunday I am glad to say. Keep it up and get quite well. God bless you.

yr. affect.
A.

The Gattis were the proprietors for the Promenade Concerts. Wren and Knight were both servants of Sullivan. Florence was Sullivan's second eldest niece who worked for a time in Sullivan's household. She was known to effectively carry out orders. Minnie Dockett was a housekeeper.

Albert Mansions
S.W.
Wednesday

Dearest Mum,

I am sorry you did not get the papers yesterday. They were sent off on Monday, but being Bank Holiday, both Wren and Knight celebrated it, and the discipline of the Mansions suffered accordingly. In future Florence says she will dispatch them herself. It is awfully hot at night conducting the Concerts, and I am glad to get home when I have finished and get to bed, for the day's work is a tiring one always. Every other day we have three hours rehearsal. How I envy you today – the picnic, fresh air, lovely scenery, and the sight of the children enjoying themselves which always does one good.

I shall try and get Gatti to let me off one night next week or the week after, so that I can run down after rehearsal and return the next afternoon.

Keep out in the air in the shade as much as you can, and you will be much stronger and better. Don't drink much fermented liquor of any kind in this heat. Lemonade is the healthiest. The less sugar the better. Now I am off to the theatre to settle Saturday's programme. Give my love to Minnie and all of the other little children. God bless you.

yr. affect
A.

The summer Promenade Concerts continued successfully. Alfred Cellier was a musical colleague of Sullivan's and a close friend. He was the Assistant Conductor for the Promenade Concerts. *H.M.S. Pinafore* opened on 25 May, 1878, and during the summer Sullivan conducted excerpts from *Pinafore* at the Promenade Concerts. This greatly increased attendance at subsequent *Pinafore* performances. John Scott Russell had developed financial problems, and there was an effort to foreclose the mortgage on his home. Edward Dicey was the editor of *The Observer*. He became one of Sullivan's closest friends and companions. He is mentioned repeatedly throughout these letters.

Aug. 16, 78
9 Albert Mansions
S.W.
Friday

Dearest Mum,

Today is an off day – no rehearsal & nothing to do 'till 3 o'clock at the theatre. So I polish off a few lines to you.

The Concerts are brilliantly successful. They never had such houses before, & the Gattis are delighted. But we work precious hard, and Cellier is a model! He is indefatigable. J.W. Davison comes regularly, & detains everyone at every corner, & tells long stories which he never finishes – but no one minds as he is so kind. Last night we did Overtura di Ballo, and tonight the Merchant of Venice. The band is getting into splendid order & some of our performances are very fine. What extraordinary weather we are having. It has been beautiful sunshine all the morning, and now suddenly there comes on heavy rain and thunder. The coolness, however, is good for the concerts and the Pinafore.

Look at today's *Times*, about poor old Scott Russell. I am dreadfully grieved, but I fear they can hold out there no longer. The marvel to me is how they have stayed so long. She will never leave the place except by force I believe. Every one is out of town, except Mrs. Chichester next door, there is no one left at any of the clubs, and so my evenings are solitary after the concert is over, but as I am always pretty tired, it doesn't matter. Edward Dicey came up last Saturday, and we had a furious bout at cribbage (my first for many months!). I beat him by 177 holes on the night! You get the papers regularly I hope, as they are sent off early always.

God bless you,
yr. affect.
A.

The mention of "Hertford" in the following letter refers to the location of Bertie's boarding school. Also, health attacks continued to give Sullivan great pain, thus the mention of eminent surgeon, Sir Henry Thompson, who was a specialist in the treatment of stones in the kidney – Sullivan's own malady. Mrs. August Dremel was a close friend of Sullivan's mother.

9 Albert Mansions
S.W.
Aug. 28, 1878
Wednesday

Dearest Mum,

I have not yet heard from Hertford about Bertie, but I expect a letter tomorrow or Friday. If it is fine tomorrow and I am well enough I will come down by the 10:15 train. But I have had two violent attacks of my old complaint Monday and today that I dread moving away from home. I was very bad indeed on Monday, and had great pain again this morning. If I don't come down tomorrow I shall go and see Thompson as I hear he goes away this week, and indeed may be gone already. Of course if it rains don't expect me. I will send a telegram. Mrs. Dremel called this morning, but I was asleep and she would have had to pass over Florence's lifeless body before she could get at me, as Florence allows no one to wake me before my time. [...]

God bless you
yr. affec.
A.

In November 1878, during the Paris Exhibition, Sullivan was made Chevalier of the Legion of Honour. He was also honored by the arrangement of a morning try-out of the *In Memoriam* overture for the Société des Concerts du Conservatoire. These concerts, the leading concert series in Paris, had never had an appearance of a British-born composer.

NEW CLUB
AVENUE MATIGNON
Sunday

Dearest Mum,

All has gone off well. My journey was without incident, and yesterday morning I was at the Conservatoire at ¼ to 9. No one there but the orchestra, the conductor, and Ambroise Thomas, & two officials. They tried the Overture twice, and when it was over the band applauded me loudly & enthusiastically. The Committee met immediately afterwards and sent me a letter last night to say that they had decided to perform it at an early date. So I have the distinction of being the first English composer performed at the Conservatoire! Ambroise Thomas has been genuinely kind and interested all through & I feel very grateful to him. Of course little Mad[ame] Montigny has been at the bottom of it. I dine with Thomas & the family tomorrow night. On Tuesday I leave for London. My time is chiefly occupied in business matters this visit [...]. God bless you. Love to all

yr. affec.
A.

George Lewis was Sullivan's friend and legal advisor.

January 12, 1879
9 Albert Mansions
Sunday night

Dearest Mum,

I have had a lot of people to see, a lot of letters to write, and a visit to George Lewis which lasted 'till past 7. Then I got some roast beef at the Garrick and was home at eight o'clock, and have been working all the evening. Florence has been ill and I thought she was sickening for something, but she is getting all right now. Matthews has attended her, and her aunt has looked after her, and I have just put her into a hot bath! At least I have made her get into one and then quickly into bed. I am sorry to hear about the measles. I hope it won't go worse than usual with children. I am sorry I missed Charlotte yesterday. I wanted to see her on her birthday.

God bless you.
yr. affect.
A. [...]

Sullivan received an honorary doctorate in music from the University of Cambridge in 1876, and was also honored by Oxford in 1879. Anglesey refers to Henry William George Paget, the third Marquess of Anglesey.

Beefsteak Club,
King William Street
Strand, W.C.

Dearest Mum,

I am going to Ascot tomorrow to stay with Anglesey. My address will be care of Marquis of Anglesey.

Coombe Meadows
Ascot

I shall be back on Friday or Saturday morning.

Enclosed is a letter from the Dean of Christ Church (Vice Chancellor of Oxford). Please take care of it & return it to me. No other musician has ever been thus honoured at both Universities!

yr. affect.
A.

Chapter Four

"Fancy your boy being underneath at the foot of Niagara..."

(In America)

Sullivan wrote just before his ship arrived in New York City. He was there for the New York opening of *The Pirates of Penzance*. For U.S. copyright reasons *Pirates* was to have its first production in the U.S. Blanche Tucker Roosevelt sang in Italian opera under the surname Rosavella, and she was to sing the role of Mabel in *Pirates.* Fred Clay was to remain Sullivan's closest friend among his fellow composers. Sullivan stayed at the New York City home of Mr. and Mrs. David Beach Grant during the first part of his stay in New York City; Suydam Grant was David Beach Grant's brother.

Cunard Steam Ship
Tuesday night
4 Nov. 1879

Dearest Mum,

Here we are at midnight, and shall be anchored in Quarantine Harbour in an hour's time for the night. In the morning we run up the bay. I land in New York about 9. The "Abyssinia" leaves early in the morning for Liverpool and this will be sent off in the mail bag. So I send just a line or two to say we are well, in good health and spirits and have had a moderate voyage. But most wonderful to relate, I have not been the least seasick! After we left Queenstown, Sunday week, we had two days of lovely weather, no sea at all, and we steamed along so fast that we thought we should be in New York on Monday (yesterday). But on Wednesday we had a sharpish gale, and the ship rolled from side to side all the day and night. The next day until yesterday we had nothing but high seas, head winds, and a good deal of rain, so that our progress was slow. Today has been lovely, and we are going ahead all night. I have enjoyed the voyage immensely as I have not been ill, and although I am weary of the everlasting ocean, I am almost sorry it is over, for it has been so pleasant.

It was a great piece of luck having the Parsons going in the same ship, and our party (4 of them, Rosavella and her husband, Gilbert, Cellier and myself) have been most cheery and happy – the envy of all the other passengers evidently. I have eaten every meal, and eaten well. There have been no exciting incidents of any sort, but the time has passed quickly and agreeably. I find I am a frustrated sailor. I am writing this in the Purser's cabin. He is a very nice fellow, by name, Wallace, and all the officers have been very nice to us. Our fellow passengers are not very interesting, but we have been independent of their attraction. It will be a curious sensation tomorrow landing in America for the first time. I suppose Suydam and Fred Clay will be at the docks to meet us, and I know I shall have a warm welcome from dear Mrs. Grant. When I get settled down this week I will write and tell you what I think about everything. Now I must shut up and go to bed, as we breakfast at 7 tomorrow morning.

My love to Charlotte and all at home. God bless you – take care of yourself.

yr. affec.
A.

I got your letters at Queenstown.

Gilbert & Sullivan's talk at the Lotus Club must have been in regard to gaining the protection of the American copyright for *Pirates* which they did not get previously for U.S. performances of *Pinafore*. Carte, of course, is Richard D'Oyly Carte, producer of the G&S operas. Sullivan's reference to codes is fascinating. Codes were needed to keep some information away from the press, and those that would take harmful advantage of G&S production rights. Several readers may not understand Sullivan's Beefsteak and Garrick reference, his attempt to explain the makeup and purpose of the Lotus Club. Sullivan's Beefsteak Club is Henry Irving's version of the 150 year old Sublime Society of Beef Steaks, a dining club founded by artists and politicians. The Garrick Club, founded in 1831, had for its purpose to "Tend to the regeneration of the Drama." Both clubs exist in different iterations today in London.

361 Twenty Third Street West
Nov. 10 1879

I hope you got my telegram dearest Mum, and understood it. By the way, if you have to telegraph to me at any time you must not address it "Sullivan, New York, but "Pinafore, New York" as there is already a Sullivan registered; so I have taken the name of Pinafore for purposes of registration. After sending you the letter to say we had arrived safely and had a fairish voyage, I thought I would allow a few days to elapse before I wrote again; so that I might look about me a little and have something to write about. Freddy, Suydam, and one or two other friends were at the dock to meet us on Wednesday morning, after undergoing the ordeal of the Custom House. I got here safely in the hands of Grant. I need scarcely say that my welcome was of the warmest and most affectionate kind. Mrs. Grant is quite unchanged – a shade stouter perhaps. Beach Grant I like immensely. He is the kindest host possible and we are great chums. I have kept tolerably quiet since my arrival, seeing a few people at dinner here only. On Saturday we dined at the Lotus Club, a sort of Garrick and Beefsteak in one. It was a splendid reception. Although both Gilbert and myself were very nervous, we spoke very well. I am told we at once gained the goodwill and sympathy of our hearers who comprised the most prominent men in New York. I send the papers containing our first "interviews", and also the account of the dinner and speeches. The *Tribune* gives our speeches verbatim. The judge of the Police Court in his speech said that to show his hearty goodwill and to mark his feeling of gratitude for the many happy hours we had given him, he hoped we might soon be brought before him as drunk and disorderly, so that he might have the satisfaction of letting us off!

Everyone is very kind and most anxious to observe every attention. The first impulse of an American when he is introduced to you is to try and do something for you – something agreeable.

I find New York very like London in most things. They, the people, are much quieter than I anticipated and have acquired a sort of English repose of manner. A few things they might with advantage adopt from us, and we many from them. Carte has arrived and has just been here – we begin rehearsing tomorrow. Things look hopeful, but of course we can't tell yet what the pecuniary result of our venture may be. I shall stay here until I return from Boston where I shall conduct the "Prodigal Son" on the 23rd. Then I go into apartments which Suydam is looking up for me.

Shall I say that Suydam is an angel? No, he is better than that, because he practices goodness, and doesn't sing about it with a harp. He is the dearest fellow in the world – so thoughtful and so unselfish.

Mrs. Grant is just as sweet and dear as she always was. She sends her love to you and says that she does her best to make me feel I have a mother here! I have a lovely room, and dressing and bathroom. The house is just as pretty as it can be, unlike a street house, more like a country cottage, and beautifully furnished. […]

Joseph is a great comfort to me. He is a most admirable servant, and is a kind, good hearted lad. He is very popular downstairs. I had a letter from Mrs. Dremel, and one from Florence yesterday – also yours came yesterday. It is very odd that I don't feel I am very far away from you all. Letters and telegrams do much. The papers tell me every morning what is doing in England; and then I think the blankness of the ocean really destroys the idea of distance; you leave one town and arrive at another just like it – same language, habits etc. The water in between prevents any division of one's thoughts – no scenery or variety or change to distract one. I assure you I don't feel nearly so far off here as I did at Nice. How is everyone? Charlotte, children, the Dremels, yourself? Don't ever telegraph unless a quick answer is required, as it is costly. In future, on any matter of joint interest, Gilbert and I will send one telegram either to you or Mrs. Gilbert with "Gallery" or "Stage" as the case may be. Keep both the codes. I don't think they clash. Now God bless you dear Mother. Everything seems bright and hopeful at present, and I hope will continue so. My love to Charlotte, and tell her that the flannel dressing gown is a great comfort to me.

yr. Loving Son,
A.

P.S.: We all drank your health on board on the 2nd – Sunday.

Sullivan moved into other lodgings on the 4th of December. D'Oyly Carte's plan in America was to perform an authentic version of *Pinafore* before the premiere performance of *Pirates* (many American productions were not faithful to the original score). The opening of this *Pinafore* was on 1st December 1879, conducted by Sullivan, at the Fifth Avenue Theatre. Chickering and Sons was an American piano manufacturer located in Boston, Massachusetts.

45 East 20th. Street
10 Dec. 1879

Dearest Mum,

Here I am in my own lodgings. I moved in last Thursday. Ground floor, two windows, with little balconies in front. An enormous sitting room and bedroom behind with large glass sliding doors in between – a large bow window in the bedroom, and beyond that a bathroom – hot and cold water etc... I am very comfortable indeed. The sitting room is a trifle too palatial perhaps, but it is very clean and also very dear. The rooms are like this

The sitting room is like two rooms without a division, except two marble pillars halfway through. Chickering has sent me a splendid grand, and I have plenty of mirrors and cupboards. I can't get any cooking done in the house, and so Joseph has bought a little gas stove, and cooks my breakfast every morning in the bathroom.

Mrs. Grant supplied me with cups, saucers, plates, knives etc., and I am perfectly independent. Joseph is an excellent fellow and does everything for me, and does it well. He is invaluable to me. He has a very nice room upstairs; and for all the rooms I have to pay 28 dollars a week (5 pound 12) and 2 dollars a week for fires, if I have them. This is considered wonderfully cheap for the neighbourhood and accommodation! But everything in New York is ruinously dear. Cabs, of which there are very few, won't look at you for any distance under a dollar. I paid 2 dollars yesterday for a trumpery wastepaper basket. A dollar is about a shilling, for all practical purposes.

I told you about our magnificent first night of the "Pinafore" here. My reception was tremendous. I sent you next day's papers. We have been going on fairly well since then, but the houses are not good enough to pay us, so we are hard at work rehearsing the new piece, as that we hope will bring great houses. I am writing night and day at the 1st. act. The 2nd is done and in rehearsal. I cannot really enjoy myself until it is produced, as I cannot go anywhere or do anything. I fear I left all my sketches of the lst act at home, as I have searched everywhere for them. I would have telegraphed for them, but they would not have arrived in time. It is a great nuisance as I have to rewrite it all now, and can't recollect every number I did. We hope to get it out in a fortnight from next Saturday – 27th. I think it will be a great success, for it is exquisitely funny, and the music is strikingly tuneful and catching.

I generally dine quietly at the Grants' every evening, and come home to work afterwards. I have declined all invitations until the piece is out. I got your letter yesterday dated the 28th. Nov., and am very happy to know all goes on well. Before you get this the girls will be home I suppose. Give my love to them, and tell them I wish they were here to answer my letters. It is as bad as London, I am obliged to have a shorthand writer. I saw the *World* notice when I was at Boston. It is very nice and flattering. Go and see the Children's "Pinafore" and tell me what you think of it. It ought to draw money. Give my love to Mrs. Dremel. I will try and write to her by Saturday's mail. I can't write anymore now. It's very late. God bless you dear Mother. Love to Charlotte and all friends.

yr. affec.
A.

The weather is extraordinary. It is so hot we can't have fires. It rains a little tonight, but it is warm. When the cold does come, however, it will doubtless come with a vengeance.

It is interesting that Gilbert was one of the *Pirates* copyists! Douglas was the son of the David Beach Grants. This letter is a good example of Sullivan's interest in giving his mother all of the details. It is assumed that "Faustin" is the artist Faustin Betbeder.

45 East 20th. St. N.Y.

Dearest Mum,

At last I am out of my penal servitude and find a little breathing time to look around me and write home. Since I last wrote to you, I have had the usual tremendous strain upon me before producing a new work, only more so. For I found that all my sketches for the 1st. Act, which I had made before leaving home, had been left behind in England, and I discovered it too late to send for them.

The 2nd. Act I brought with me complete, so they set to work rehearsing that, whilst I wrote the 1st. act. Then I had the whole opera to score, of course, so that the last three weeks have been imprisonment with hard labour – never going to bed before 5:30 in the morning, sometimes later. However, it was finished at last, even the Overture, and brought out the night before last with a success unparalleled in New York, as our telegram will have told you. We had long and wearisome rehearsals, but fortunately our Company and all the chorus are charming people and devoted to us, and spared themselves no pains or trouble to do this work thoroughly well – all except the tenor who is an idiot – vain and empty headed. He very nearly upset the piece on the first night, as he didn't know his words and forgot his music. We shall, I think, have to get rid of him. On Tuesday night there was a full dress rehearsal to which most of the press and a few personal friends were invited. To my surprise, it all went very smoothly indeed, and those who were there were wildly enthusiastic. It was over at <u>one</u>, and then I came home, and, assisted by Clay and Gilbert as copyists, Cellier and I finished the overture – I got to bed at 5, and was up again at 9 for a band rehearsal. I was dreadfully ill all day. I could hardly hold up my head – it ached and burnt like iron. I could eat nothing and when I went into the orchestra at 8, I felt more dead than alive; and I looked so, everyone told me. When the curtain went up after the overture I began to pull myself together, and thought only of the piece. There was no doubt about its success. We took nine encores, and might have had more if I had liked. The laughter and applause continued through the whole piece until the very end, and then there were thunder calls for Gilbert and myself after every act. Its success was undoubted and instantaneous, and the next day (yesterday) both performances (being New Year's Day there was a matinee as well) were crowded, and the booking is already a fortnight ahead.

We anticipate immense business for the next few weeks. At the end of the eighth week from now, we leave New York, and go round to the big towns west. Chicago, Cincinnati, St. Louis etc. where good business is to be done.

We [will] also send out another Company with it, as soon as we can get it ready, to the smaller towns – in New England first, then south. Strike whilst the iron is hot. How long we shall stay ourselves in America, I don't know. It depends of course upon business. I don't think I shall stay one week longer than necessary. That you may depend upon. We may go across to San Francisco, as there is money to be made there.

What do I think of the piece myself? The libretto is ingenious, clear, wonderfully funny in parts, and sometimes brilliant in dialogue – beautifully written for music, as is all Gilbert does, and all the action and business perfect.

The music is infinitely superior in every way to the Pinafore – tunier and more developed, of a higher class altogether. I think that in time it will be more popular. The *mise en scène* and the dresses are something to be dreamed about! I never saw such beautiful combinations of colour and form on any stage. All the girls are dressed in the old fashioned English style. Every dress designed separately by Faustin, and some of the girls look as if they had stepped bodily out of the frame of a Gainsborough picture. In New York ladies are raving about them. The Policemen's chorus is an enormous hit, and they are cheered tremendously when they march on with their Bull's Eyes all alight, and are always encored. I am sanguine of its success in London, for there all the local allusions etc. will have twice the force they have here. I send you all the morning papers except the *Sun* which is excellent also. There is not a copy to be had. You will see that they don't go into the music much, as they don't know much about it, and it isn't printed.

So the New Year opens auspiciously for me. I have been nowhere, and seen hardly anyone since I wrote. I dined on Christmas with the Grants of course. Douglas was at home for his holidays, and we had a pleasant family dinner. I came home to work at ll. After the performance on New Year's Eve I went home with them to drink the Old Year out, and we didn't forget you of course.

Yesterday being my first free day, and a fine one, I drove about all the afternoon leaving cards, and making calls, trying to atone for my past faults in that respect. Next week I go to Baltimore to the "Grand Welcome Concert" given to me, which I conduct. [...] Don't address your letters <u>here</u>, as I may leave these lodgings next week – I don't much care for them. They are large and not very comfortable. – Address either to Mrs. Grant's or to the "New York Club" of which I am a member. Mrs. Grant's is perhaps the best. Write and tell me all that is going on at home – how you all spent Christmas and the New Year; what you think of the "Children's Pinafore" (which I hear is an enormous success), how the girls are etc. D'Oyly is here and sends his kindest regards to you, Charlotte and the children. God bless you all.

yrs. affec.
A.

The Academy of Music Concert in Baltimore, Maryland was advertised as having the "largest orchestra heard in Baltimore." Sullivan's music performed at the concert, along with Beethoven and Wagner, included the *Overtura di Ballo*, and music to *The Tempest* and *The Merchant of Venice.* There were also songs – including *The Lost Chord* with Sullivan at the piano. Leo Wheat was a pianist and composer who had been a fellow-student of Sullivan at Leipzig. Ernest Ford was later engaged as arranger of the piano part of Sullivan's opera, *Ivanhoe*, for the vocal score, and also conducted performances of *Ivanhoe.* Ford's Opera House opened in Baltimore in 1871. It earned a solid reputation with its Shakespearean productions.

Mount Vernon Hotel
Baltimore
Thursday night
8 Jan. 1880

Dearest Mum,

Here I am, the concert is over, and I have to be up at six tomorrow morning to go off by a 7:10 train. So, before going to bed, I write a line for Saturday's steamer, to tell you that all has gone well, and that I am delighted with the Baltimorites.

I left New York yesterday morning at 9, and arrived here about 3. Was met by some of the Committee at the station, and went straight to rehearsal which lasted 'till six. I found the band rather rough as a matter of course, but we got things a little into shape, and well prepared for another rehearsal this morning. After dinner at the hotel, I had a reception in my room, to which a number of gentlemen came – Committee, press etc. Then I went to Ford's Opera House. They got hold of it that I was there and cheered me tremendously, so that I had to go on the stage and bow.

After that, I went to the "Wednesday Club", a most charming place, where they have a large concert room, stage etc. I was most hospitably entertained there by a great number of "our prominent citizens", and then came home. Today, I have been rehearsing, driving with Ford in the Druid Hill Park, and then home to dinner. D'Oyly Carte came over from New York to keep me company, and after the concert we went to the Maryland Club with a number of gentlemen to supper. Now I am home dead tired. The Academy of Music was crowded with a brilliant audience, and the music went very well, a good many things were encored, and I got a great reception.

I will send you papers and a programme. Tomorrow morning I am going off with Carte to stay with our old friend, Leo P. Wheat, who has a fine farm in Virginia. I want to see a bit of Virginian country life, so eagerly embraced this opportunity. We return here on Saturday to a ladies reception and dramatic performance at the "Wednesday Club", and go back to New York on Sunday. The "Pirates of Penzance" is still doing enormous business every night, and is likely to last; so that at last I really think I shall get a little money out of America. I ought to, for they have made a good deal out of me.

We are going to send out two companies, one for New England and another for the south – Washington, Baltimore etc. Strike whilst the iron is hot. I have left my lodgings, as the landlady was always drunk and abusive, and have left all my things at the Grant's. When I return I must seek for fresh apartments, so write always to Mrs. Grant's house, or to the "New York Club" where I go every day. Now I must go to bed for four hours. God bless you all. My love to all.

yr. affec.
A.

In the following letter, Lord Lorne was Governor General of Canada, serving as the representative of the Queen of Great Britain. Sullivan did visit Lord Lorne in Ottawa, Canada, before leaving the United States. Samuel Barlow was a lawyer friend of Gilbert's. François Cellier, Alfred's brother, was also a close musical associate of Sullivan. Sullivan consistently continues to provide for his deceased brother's family. The Marquess of Anglesey died six days before this letter, at Albert Mansions. It may be helpful to note that the name "Albert Mansions" stood for a series of apartment blocks, with "mansion flats" of three and four bedrooms with servants' quarters. Thus, the Marquess was a neighbour of Sullivan's. The "Dominion Hymn" was a poem written by Lord Lorne, who asked Sullivan to set the words to music, anticipating that it would become the Canadian national anthem. French Canadians objected, and the effort was abandoned.

Hoffman House
New York
6 Feb. 1880

Dearest Mum,

I suppose you think that my hard work is over, and so I can write oftener. On the contrary, my work at present is harder than ever. The success of the "Pirates" is so great that there is naturally a demand for it all over the States. So we have to organize companies, rehearse them and send them about. You may imagine what it is when I tell you that, in the four companies which we have at present in hand, there are 40 principals, 140 chorus and 78 band, besides conductors, all of which have to be selected, approved and rehearsed by us. Then there are all the staff connected with the management, like treasurers etc.

I rehearsed 10 and ½ hours on Monday, and 8 hours every other day this week. The Philadelphia company opens on Monday next, and we have a very fine troupe. Cellier has been there all the week rehearsing chorus, band etc. Gilbert went over on Wednesday morning and stays there. I go over tomorrow.

I was obliged to stay here to get on with the rehearsals for the southern and western companies. Two separate companies a day to rehearse! But, of course, it means money, and so I don't mind the work. But, I don't like people to think I have a rattling good time of it. I conduct at Philadelphia the first night of course, and return here Tuesday morning for rehearsals. The southern company starts out on Monday the 16th, and the western one on Friday the 20th.

I received a letter from Lord Lorne yesterday begging me to come and stay with them before I left the New World. So, I have written to say I will go about the 23rd, <u>for I must break the news to you</u> that I return by the "Gallia" on the 3rd. of March, and hope to be at home again about the 14th or 15th. I have given up Cuba and the western states, as we <u>must</u> produce the "Pirates" in London without delay. Otherwise, the best part of the season will escape us. So, duty first, pleasure afterwards.

I am very sorry to leave now, just as the hard work is over and I might enjoy myself a little. I am much happier than I was; am used to things which rubbed me up the wrong way at first, and am beginning to get fond of this place and the people, or some of them at least.

My rooms are very comfortable though expensive, and I have friends whose houses are always open to me. People like the Barlows, Woolseys, Perkins etc. Tonight I dined at the Grants, as I generally do when not invited out – only Beach and Mrs. Grant & myself. Although I have moved, I keep a latch key and go in & out when I like. I telegraphed to F. Cellier this morning to try and find the hymn (words and music) I wrote to Lord Lorne's words – about Canada. I left it in England, of course, having carefully put it aside to bring with me. I hope he will find it.

Tell the girls with my love, I was very pleased indeed to get their letters. I can't answer them myself, as I cannot find time to get my business correspondence done. I will send you all the papers from Philadelphia and a telegram about the reception of the piece. As I shall be home so soon now, I think I would rather that Amy didn't go away 'till my return. I will then see after her and probably take her over to Paris myself. (Your letter of the 24th arrived this morning.) If we continue so successful here, and she is a good girl, I will see what can be done about placing her in a good school there. Give my love to Charlotte and all the children. I hope she got my letter I wrote to her. I meant to write on her birthday, but couldn't, and forgot all about it when I wrote! God bless you dear Mother.

yr. affec.
A.

Poor dear old Anglesey's death was a great shock to me. I read it in the papers and immediately telegraphed to you. Keep all the newspapers and cuttings I send you.

On his way to Ottawa, Canada, Sullivan stopped on the Canadian side of Niagara Falls. After describing his reaction to the Falls, Sullivan mentions his work environment, using a descriptive word that is completely and appropriately unacceptable in contemporary use. We leave the word intact for accuracy.

Prospect House
Niagara Falls
Canada
23 Feb. 1880

Dearest Mum,

Here I am seated at my window watching the great Niagara dashing and foaming within fifty yards of me. The morning is fine, bright and cold – snow covering the ground, making the sunshine all the more dazzling. At first, I was disappointed in the great cataract, as everyone is. It did not seem so large and mighty as I had imagined it. But nearer acquaintance changes that opinion; and every moment it becomes more and more stupendous. In summer I have no doubt it is very beautiful; but I am sure that winter is the time when it is finest. The river is frozen over for the first time since 1865; and yesterday we walked across it. We also went under the falls with guides and proper tarpaulin dresses! What do you think of that? Fancy your boy being underneath at the foot of Niagara with the great foaming, tumbling cataract falling just in front of him! You wouldn't have slept, would you! Just as I look up now it is magnificent. You can't see much below the fall as there is an immense cloud of spray always there; but the water, spray, snow and sunshine make a glorious combination. This is my first day of rest for a very long time. Up 'till Friday last, the day we started, we worked night and day like niggers. We started the 3rd Company last Monday. I went to Newark with them to conduct and give them a good send off. It was a great success – crowded house; and that company is doing very well indeed – good business everywhere it goes. Then on Monday we had only the Western Company to look after, and set to work rehearsing every day and night. It isn't only the rehearsals that take up time. It is the whole of the details which are so worrying – band parts, conductor parts to get ready, conductors to teach, and a thousand things that no one outside dreams of. However, we got all in order and finished our last dress rehearsal at 4 last Friday. Then came a hurry, scurry to get off by the 6 train – people, dresses, music, baggage. I called at Mrs. Grant's on my way to the station, got a mouthful of food, and at six we left New York for Buffalo, where the Company was to give a morning and evening performance. The Company consisted of about 60 altogether, with Gilbert, Carte and myself. We three had a sleeping section to ourselves.

We arrived at Buffalo at 8 on Saturday morning in a violent snowstorm. Of course our first thought was "Bad house this morning". We played at 2, and it wasn't a very good house nor was it a good performance – everyone was nervous, and made mistakes. But at night the house was crammed, and it went very well. Gilbert and I got a big reception and everyone seemed pleased.

We bid goodbye to our company in the morning, as they were going on to Cincinnati to play this week. We three "bosses" took train to Niagara, about an hour from Buffalo. Then we took carriages at the station and drove over the suspension bridge to this (the Canada) side, and wandered about on foot, and bought photographs, dined (excellent dinner at 1 o'clock), saw everything there was to see by driving and walking. At 5, Gilbert and Carte went back by train to New York where they will arrive this morning. I came back to the hotel, feeling very dreary and alone, and miserable at the prospect of spending 24 hours here without a soul I knew. I am on my way to Ottawa, and there is no train 'till 3 this afternoon. I arrive in Ottawa at 6:20 tomorrow morning. Fortunately I found the landlord and his wife, pleasant, agreeable people, and so I spent the evening in their sitting room. This is a delightful, little hotel, clean, comfortable, and the food the best I have eaten in America. My room is a corner one facing the Falls, and I can see them under every aspect.

I am writing this early in the morning as I can't dress yet, my trunk having been left behind at Buffalo. Joseph has gone over for it, and so I must wait 'till he returns. I shall stay at Ottawa 'till Saturday, then post haste back to New York to pack up, say goodbye to everyone, and start Wednesday morning the 3rd

March at 10 a.m. in the "Gallia". Look out in the papers for her arrival at Queenstown. I will telegraph you from there. Tell Florence to be on the look out and have everything comfortable and ready whatever time we arrive at Liverpool. I shall come straight up to town, so it might be four o'clock in the morning when I arrive. I shall have been away five months! To me it has gone like lightning, but I have never had an idle moment 'till this morning.

Now, goodbye. God bless you, love to Charlotte and the chicks. Thank Mrs. Dremel and Minnie for their letters. I have not had a moment to write to them, but they will excuse that I am sure.

yr. affec.
A.

P.S. This is not the shortest way from New York to Ottawa, only, as I wanted to go to Buffalo and see Niagara, I made one journey of it.

Princess Louise was the Governor-General's wife, and daughter of Queen Victoria. Sullivan's mother must have found the hymn Sullivan had written for Lord Lorne and sent the missing materials. The hymn was published in Montreal and London. Sullivan decided to include a little sketch of his toboggan experience.

Government House
Ottawa
Wednesday
25 Feb. 1880

Dearest Mum,

I wrote you a long letter from Niagara the day before yesterday, so don't expect another now. I only write to say that I left Niagara at 3:30 on Monday afternoon and arrived here at 7 yesterday morning. When I got into the train the weather was mild and sunshiny. When I got out, the sun was shining brilliantly, but oh! The cold! A sleigh was at the station to meet me, and in the short drive up to here, about a mile, the skin was nearly taken off my face. I realized for the first time what Canada was. Today it is much milder, but there is no sun. It is muggy and depressing. The poor Princess is not out of her room yet, and only got up yesterday for the first time, and for a very short period. She has had a dreadfully bad accident: her face cut, her head knocked about, and her ear torn so much that it had to be sewn up. She is getting better, thank God, but she is very low and depressed. It is sad and unfortunate in every way. I had looked forward so much to being constantly with her, and now I shall see but very little of her.

We went Toboggoning [sic] yesterday afternoon, my first experience. It is exhilarating but "jumpy", as I went whizzing through the air at the rate of 60 miles an hour. I wasn't sure whether I had got my body on, or left it behind. It is easily explained. You sit in a flat sledge, and are then sent down an inclined plane, either natural, a hillside for instance, or a made one. You go on until the sledge stops of its own accord on level ground.

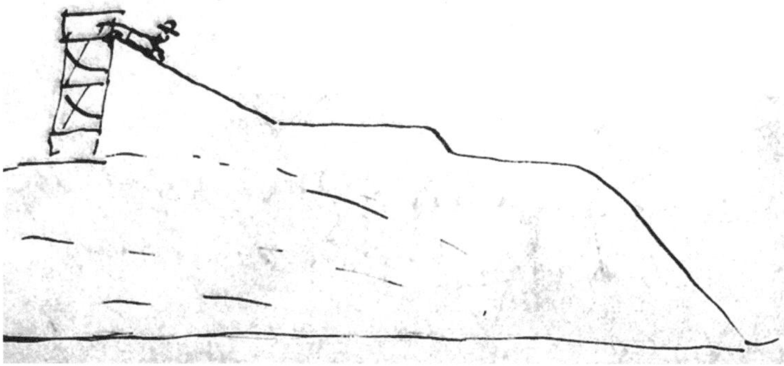

I got your last letter this morning, forwarded from the Grant's. Also the music and words of Canada's hymn. It was very clever of you to find it. I shan't write again before I leave, so this is my last letter from America. I leave here Saturday morning, arrive in New York same time Sunday. I wake Monday and Tuesday to visits, business, bills etc. and sail in the "Gallia" at 10a.m. Wednesday morning. I will telegraph from Queenstown, if possible. God bless you all.

yr. affec.
A

Sullivan as a Chapel Royal chorister

Sullivan, aged 18, in Leipzig

Sullivan in 1864, Birmingham Festival

Mary Clementina Coghlan Sullivan, Sullivan's mother

Frederic Thomas Sullivan, Sullivan's brother

Charlotte Louisa Lacy Sullivan,
Frederic's wife and Sullivan's sister-in-law

William Lacy, Sr.

Amy Sophia Sullivan Stephens,
Sullivan's eldest niece

Amy Sophia Sullivan, Sullivan's niece,
as a young lady before her marriage, wearing the
necklace Sullivan bought for her in Egypt

Florence Louise Sullivan, Sullivan's niece, as a young lady, wearing the necklace Sullivan bought for her in Egypt

Charles M. Stevens

Arthur Seymour Sullivan

Maud Helen Sullivan Lacy.
Sullivan's niece

Maud and Richard Lacy at the time of their marriage

Frederic Richard (Dickie) Sullivan, Sullivan's nephew

Arthur Seymour Sullivan and Herbert (Bertie) Sullivan, his nephew

Arthur Seymour Sullivan

Arthur Seymour Sullivan, photographed near the end of his life

Chapter Five

"We shall wish you all happiness for the New Year, though, just as if you were here."

(Back Home, Then Travel Correspondent)

In the following letter, "Dick" refers to Sullivan's second eldest nephew, Richard Frederic Sullivan (born 1872). Sullivan has obviously returned home from his trip to the United States, and writes to Dick at his school in Margate, Kent.

9. Albert Mansions
S.W.
24 March 1880

My dear Dick,

Yes – I am safe at home again, having come 3000 miles across the ocean. Isn't that a lot of water! I don't think I shall be able to come down to Margate, as I have so much to do, but if I can, I will. I hope you are a good boy, and are working hard at your lessons. If so, I shall be pleased, and you like me to be pleased, don't you?

yr. affect. uncle
Arthur

I enclose 2 shillings for you.
A.

Sullivan searched for a school for his eldest niece, Amy, in France. He finally selected a school in Paris. Pauline Viardot-Garcia was a celebrated mezzo soprano.

Hotel du Rhin
Thursday

Dearest Mum,

I didn't leave this morning, and I am not going away from here 'till Sunday, as I have important business with Mad[ame] Viardot. I was obliged to change my plans last night. I have made many enquiries about schools, and have been over the whole of Paris inspecting different ones. I liked none of them. I heard yesterday of one at Fontainebleau, which from all accounts seems excellent. It is only an hour from Paris, and if it is fine I shall run out there tomorrow and see it. If you and Charlotte would like some gloves send me "number" and description and I will get them Saturday.

Write by return. Love to all

yr. affect.
A.

The work to which Sullivan refers is his sacred musical drama, *The Martyr of Antioch*, performed at the Leeds Festival in 1880. Emma Albani is the name of the celebrated Canadian-born soprano. She was one of Sullivan's favorite sopranos, and one of the best interpreters of his music.

1 Albert Mansions
S.W.

9 Sept. 1880

Dearest Mum,

I have finished my work, thank God, but am now in the midst of proofs, copyists etc., so that I can't get away. I might get a run next week, but I don't know what to do.

It is of no use going on the Continent as I have not much time, and there is nowhere in England I care to go to. I might take it into my head to run through Boulogne next Tuesday, and will let you know beforehand.

Why doesn't Amy write to me occasionally? She never tells me of her life or doings, or what interests her, or strikes her. You tell me many interesting little details – but she ought to write – naturally and freely without straining after smartness or originality. I have not heard from Charlotte since I told you. London is very empty – no one in town. I wrote all day Sunday (as I got a telegram from Albani asking me not to come to Gloucester), dined alone at the Club – not a soul there, and came home and wrote all night! I have shipped Jack [Sullivan's servant] off to the Cape today. I hope he will get work to do there. God bless you.

yr. affec.
A

On the 15th of September, 1880, Sullivan left England to visit a Belgian health spa for his digestion and liver ailments. He includes some interesting advice as to the drinking of wine. Amy was attending school near Paris (Neuilly). Madame Bazault must be a representative of the school.

Hotel de Flandre
A Spa
TENU PAR SURY PÉRE PROPRIÉTAIRE

Sunday morning

I was very glad to get your letter and find you were all right and comfortable. I heard from Charlotte the night before I left England enclosing the girls' school bills. She said she was dull down there. She also told me she didn't think you took enough of some nourishment in the way of wine. Pray, don't fail to take what is really good and strengthening regularly. A pint of good wine every day you ought to have. English beer never agrees with people abroad, as the climate is so much lighter. So I don't advise you to take that; but good wine you ought to take. It is very dull here. There is nothing to do but to walk out, & I do that every day with the Parsons, & we dine together every night. I shall leave here Tuesday or Wednesday morning, sleep one night in Paris & come on to Boulogne the next day. I will telegraph to you, & you must order me a bedroom & sitting room, & a room for Silva who is with me. If you can't get it in your hotel, get it near you.

Of course get Amy what she wants. I have paid Mad[ame] Bazault's bill which by the bye, includes several articles of clothing – only as these things are a mystery to me, I never attempt to fathom them. Good bye – God bless you.

yr. affec.
A.

Prince Christian was the Danish husband of the third daughter of Queen Victoria, Princess Helena. Sullivan's invitation to breakfast is just another small example of his companionship and loyalty to his mother.

Wednesday night

Dearest Mum,

I have been all day at Cambridge and have done my work there like a man. I have only had a chop today, as Thompson won't let me eat or drink much. I came home from Paris late Monday night – we were very late indeed and had a beastly passage. Yesterday from 10 in the morning (when I went to see Prince Christian) until I went to bed, I literally had not a moment free from active work – today I have seen Thompson again, and been to Cambridge and tomorrow night must go back to Paris, as the Prince of Wales particularly begged me to, in order to settle some business. I shall probably return with him Saturday or Sunday night.

I want you to come up tomorrow morning and see me, as I shall be free 'till one o'clock, after that I shall have half a dozen different men on business.

Have a cup of tea early and breakfast here at ten. We shall be quiet and undisturbed. I hope all is well.

God bless you
yr. affec.
A.

Menu
Fried Sole
Bacon
Jam
Toast
Tea or coffee

Sullivan was a good friend of the Duke of Edinburgh. The Duke gave him the opportunity of a sea cruise and a visit to Russia in the summer of 1881. Walter Smythe was Sullivan's secretary. Sir W. Hewitt is Admiral Sir William Hewitt. The Empress' mother is the Queen of Denmark. "Levitsky's" refers to the photography studio of Count Sergei Lvovich Levitsky. The Levitsky studio had been awarded the title Photographer of the Royal Majesty just four years prior. "Maréchal de la Cour" translates as "Marshall of the Court." The Emperor of Russia was Alexander III. His father, Alexander II, had been assassinated only four months prior to this letter.

Alexandria Peterhoff
Wednesday 6 July 1881

Dearest Mum,

We got a mail bag yesterday morning, the first since leaving England, but to my disappointment there was no letter from you. Smythe wrote, and as he said nothing to the contrary, I presume that everything and everybody is well. I hope you got my letter written after I left Copenhagen. [...] There was nothing of any interest happening afterwards except an entertainment we got up for the ship's crew – artists, H.R.H. The Duke of Edinburgh, three sailors, Major Welch (commanding the Marines), Mr. F. Clay and Mr. Arthur Sullivan. It went off splendidly, and to finish with I sang "The Englishman" from the Pinafore, and the whole crew to my astonishment sang the chorus!

We arrived at Cronstadt on Saturday afternoon, but did not land 'till Sunday morning. There was a tremendous lot of saluting, guns firing, flags waving, and officials in cocked hats coming on board etc., and we gave them all champagne.

The Duke, Sir W. Hewitt, Clay, myself and the two aides-de-camp steamed away in a little launch past Cronstadt, up the Neva to Peterhoff, a village about 15 miles (I think) from St. Petersburg. Here are all the summer palaces of the Emperor and all the Grand Dukes. It is like an enormous park, with a mixture of the Bois de Boulogne and Virginia Water. The gardens about the Palace are lovely and have beautiful fountains in them. Close to the Palace is our villa, a spare one belonging to the Emperor where he put up stray royalties and relations when they came to see him. It is very comfortable but plainly furnished. The bedrooms like an alpine hotel – polished floors and no carpets. There is a first rate cook and staff of servants, and we are as jolly and happy as possible. Monday we spent in driving about [...].

In the evening we dined at the Palace with the Emperor and Empress. There were 46 at dinner: high dignitaries, Royal Family and ourselves in court dress. The Emperor and Empress both spoke to me. The former shook hand and said "nous sommes souvent rencontrés a Londres", and the Empress said her mother had written to her about me, and told her I was going to give her some music. I made the acquaintance of a lot of swell officials and had a pleasant time of it. Yesterday we steamed up to St. Petersburg and went straight to the Winter Palace to lunch – more officials and more presentations. After lunch we went all over the Palace, certainly the finest in Europe. It is enormous in size and as a rule very fine, and in good taste. Such magnificent suites of rooms and not one, but five or six splendid ball and concert rooms. I was very much impressed by it. Then we called on the English minister, Mr. Wyndham – drove to see the spot where the Emperor was assassinated (a temporary shrine is erected there), went to be photographed at Levitsky's, drove about the town which is very empty and very gloomy, and returned to dine at the Winter Palace. The town is handsome, but certainly not lively, of course allowance must be made for it's being out of the season; and I daresay in winter there is a good deal of life and gaiety, but at present what with the dull time of the year, the general mourning, and a universal look of depression, it is not very cheerful. We returned home here after dinner, played a rubber and went to bed. This morning we started again at 9 and went to the Winter Palace to hear famed Imperial Chapel Choir, who were all in full dress, red and gold, waiting for us. The Duke said to me, "Doesn't it remind you of when you were in the Chapel Royal?" And it did rather. There were about 80, and blasé as I am with music, I confess to a new sensation at hearing them. It is like nothing else. They have basses with the most wonderful voices going down to the <u>low A</u>, and the effect of their singing their church music was thrilling. Sometimes it was exactly like an organ, only more beautiful. They sang for an hour, and I could have heard them for a couple of hours more. Then we went to lunch again, and after lunch returned home here. Tonight the Duke dined with the Czar, and we were invited to dine at the Palace with the Maréchal de la Cour (Prince Galitzin) [...]. Hewitt sat on his right, and I on his left. We had a very pleasant dinner, short and sweet, and then returned home. The other things besides the choir which have impressed me most are the caviar and the sterlet! I never knew what caviar was until I ate it fresh here, and as for the sterlet! Well, it is an etherealized eel, it melts in your mouth. So you see, we are having a "real lovely time of it".

Tomorrow, as the Duke is engaged all day, [Fred] Clay and I are going in to St. Petersburg by ourselves to potter about. We take a German servant of the Emperors with us, as we can't speak a word of Russian, and the Duke, who is kindness itself, has ordered one of the Imperial carriages to meet us and take us about all day. I shall take this letter to the Embassy, and give it to Stevens (Queen's messenger) who leaves tomorrow, so you will get it I hope on Monday. We leave here on Saturday or Sunday, and you can write to me to Kiel, where we hope to be on the following Thursday. Address to me "Care of H.R.H. The Duke of Edinburgh, Royal Reserve Squadron, Kiel, Germany". It will reach me all right. I hope all is well, and everything going all right. My love to Charlotte and the children. God bless you.

yr. affec.
A.

Soon after his Russian trip, Sullivan, attended a German spa (he had a recurrence of his kidney problem). Here, under medical supervision, he drank the waters.

47 Untere Promenade
Homburg – Frankfurt
Wednesday 17 Aug. 1881

Dearest Mum,

You see that there can be no mistake as to the date of this letter. I have been here three days now, having arrived late Saturday night. Sunday I passed in seeing the doctor, & looking for lodgings. I found these and moved into them on Monday, after Dicey left for Kissingen. They are very pleasant & comfortable, and I think I shall get on very well.

To my amazement I found that the Coutts Lindsays were here. He has gone back to England for the Edinburgh Volunteer Review, & she is left here with her two girls. I went to see her yesterday before dinner, & found her very weak. She doesn't seem to get any strength at all. There are very few people I know. […] I get up at 7:15 (don't be startled!) every morning, so as to be at the Spring at 8. I drink a glass of filthy water, walk about for a quarter of an hour, drink another glass, walk for three quarters of an hour, then come in to breakfast at 9 – my breakfast consists only of coffee & rusks, and of course as I am nearly starving by that time, having eaten nothing since dinner the evening before, I think it the most delicious meal of the day. After breakfast I sit a while & read or write until luncheon at 12:30 – then I have a cutlet & vegetables – nothing to drink & a delicious cup of cocoa afterward. Then I walk for 2 or three hours & take a glass of water from another spring at 4. Ink & Lucifer matches seem to be the principal ingredients of the waters judging by the taste. Then my work for the day is over, & I dine at the Kursaal at ½ past 6, lounge about listening to the Band, & go to bed about 11. Yesterday was a pouring wet day, so I couldn't walk much, & it poured all this morning, but it is clearing up now I think, so I shall get my afternoon exercise probably. This Arcadian life is to go on for three weeks. What becomes of me then the doctor only knows.

The Grand Duke of Mecklenburgh (blind) is here, & was good enough to send for me to be presented to him. I generally sit with him at his table after dinner & chat – a party of 6 or 7 of us.

Now I must finish this. Write and tell me how things are going. Give my love to Charlotte who I hope is better. I expected to hear from Amy. It is a miserably dull existence here, especially when it rains, but I don't mind so long as I have books. God bless you
yr. affec. A.

Once the G&S opera *Patience* was established at the Savoy Theatre, Sullivan decided to travel with his journalist friend, Edward Dicey, to Egypt. Dicey was combining business with pleasure, as he was also a director of the Ottoman Bank in Cairo.

In December of 1881 a marriage occurred which one might think would have changed Sullivan's responsibility to Charlotte. Four years after Frederic's death, Charlotte Sullivan remarried, becoming the wife of Benjamin Hutchinson, who was thirteen years younger than herself. Her husband had difficulty finding a job, so Sullivan continued to be the main support of the family.

Hotel des Pays Bas
Port Said
31 Dec. 1881

Dearest Mum,

I hope you got the letter I wrote you last week posted at Naples on Tuesday. We arrived there at daybreak on Tuesday morning, and as it was a lovely morning, Dicey and I rose early and went on shore at seven o'clock. The town was alive and we sent telegrams, bought Lucifer matches etc. and drove about until 8:30 when we returned to the ship, as we were to depart again at 9. I cannot give you my impressions in a letter, but I can truly say that "See Naples and die" is not quite without reasonable foundation as a boast. The town and bay are divinely beautiful especially in the morning sun as we saw them.

When we left Naples, nothing of interest happened. We skirted the Calabrian coast, rocky and wild, passed through the Straits of Messina at midnight, then saw no land 'till we passed Crete on Thursday afternoon. Then no land again 'till we arrived here about 6 this morning. I dressed quickly, went on deck and looked at Egypt for the first time. There wasn't very much to see, as the town is a new, ramshackling place, rather like a Californian "City" in its unsubstantial character; but the ship was surrounded by small boats each containing one or two dirty, picturesque Arabs – coal boats etc., and all gesticulating and making an infernal din. Dicey and I said goodbye to our shipmates most of whom were going on to India, China etc., and we came ashore. We are obliged to stay here all today – start tomorrow morning at 7:30 in the Canal Steamer which will take us as far as Ismaila. There we have to sleep tomorrow night and go on by train on Monday to Cairo. It is a monstrous shame that we can't get there quicker, but it is done on purpose, every obstacle being thrown in the way of travellers going to Cairo by Port Said instead of Alexandria.
Dicey and I will have to see the old year out in this heaven forsaken place all alone. We shall get a bottle of champagne and try to think we are rollicking dogs. We shall wish you all happiness for the New Year, though, just as if you were here. Kiss all the chicks for me and Charlotte. My kindest regards to Hutchinson, and in return drink my health, but not in Ironsides finest old claret. God bless you dearest Mother. I will write again when I am well settled down at Cairo. Tell Smythe to send me the "Sporting and Dramatic Illustrated" every week with the other papers I ordered.

yr. affec.
A.

A statement made by Arthur Jacobs in his book, *Arthur Sullivan a Victorian Musician* affirms our belief that Sullivan had the ability to write fine letters. We quote from Jacobs: "The Egyptian trip indeed brought out Sullivan's genius – it is hardly too strong a word – for letter-writing. Lively observation of unfamiliar scenes, witty and sometimes self-depreciating accounts of his activities, shrewd professional assessment – all are there, but always with a caring remembrance of those at home." The "new home" referred to a home within a new block of flats called Queen's Mansions. Sullivan took Nº 1. This was on the same street as Albert Mansions. Tigrane Bey was a leading Egyptian official. It is assumed that "Prince Osman" refers to Abdul Hamid II, the 34th Sultan of the Ottoman Empire ("The House of Osman"). His oldest son, Prince Şehzade Mehmed Selim Osmanoğlu Efendi Constantinople, was only 12 at the time of Sullivan's visit.

Shepherd's Hotel, Cairo
16 Jan. 1882

Dearest Mum,

I was very glad to get your letter through Smythe and to know that things were all right. I have sent the fullest instructions about the new house, and so Smythe and Clark can be going ahead.

Since I wrote last week, I have made another excursion – viz: to Sakkara. We took donkeys with us and the donkey boys, as we had a long ride when we got out of the train. We got out at Beschredeyer (an hour from Cairo) and mounted our donkeys, and a very imposing procession we made. We had a lovely ride of an hour and a half through villages built on the site of ancient Memphis, palm groves etc. 'till we got to the Great Desert and the ruins of Sakkara. There we saw several pyramids including the "step" pyramid (built in steps).

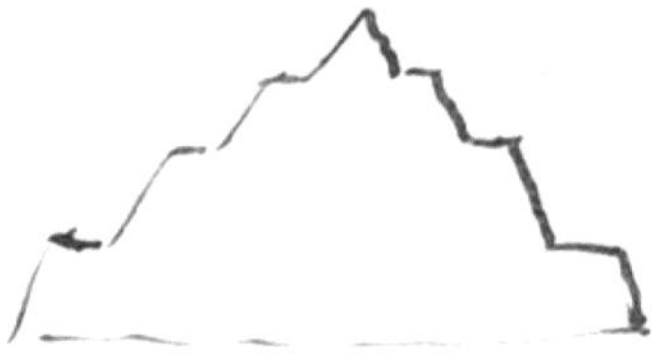

The Serapeum, or tombs of the sacred bulls and the tomb of Ti. I can't give you a description of all these, or their history. Murray or Baedeker's Egypt will tell you all about everything. We lunched there, and after more exploring returned home. The ride home I enjoyed the most I think. The villages, palm groves, Arabs, women, camels, flocks etc., all made a scene of picturesque beauty that only a painter could reproduce. We got home at seven, tired but well pleased with our excursions. The palm is the most beautiful of all trees, and gives an oriental look to the country at once.

On Saturday night a concert of real Arab music was got up for me at Tigrane Bey's by him and Prince Osman. The six most distinguished musicians in Egypt were engaged and for four hours I listened to them – two sang, the others played. One, on a sort of large mandolin called "Ud". One a kind of trichord zither called a "Kanoun" – both instruments played with a quill, the third a perpendicular flute called "Nei", and from which I could not extract a single sound [...] and the fourth tapped a tambourine lightly. We all sat about on divans and smoked cigarettes and cried "Allah" (God, or bravo!) when they played or sang anything more ugly (to our ears) than usual. They only stopped once during the evening for a few minutes, otherwise they went on ceaselessly, running one thing into another, or at least seeming to do so. It was very strange, but to a certain degree fascinating; but, although I had four hours of it, I cannot recollect one single phrase or bit of rhythm even now. I must hear it two or three times, then perhaps I may be able to note it down a little. I enjoy the great advantage of having heard the best real Arab music, and I was certainly surprised at the way the leader played the "Ut" (pronounced oot). He had marvellous execution and is a really fine player. Prince Osman lamented the fact that he was the only one now and that there is no one to succeed him. [...]

I patter about the bazaars every day, but as yet have bought nothing particular – if anything is very old and very good it is sure to be very dear.

There are not many visitors here this year, and it is not so warm as usual; indeed yesterday was a bitterly cold day, the coldest they have had for some years. Still there is always bright sunshine. I know most of the residents now, and feel quite at home. Write and tell me what you are doing in London. Now that Charlotte and the two girls are away, it must be very quiet for you, and I am very glad Miss Bartoldeci is staying with you. As you know I do not like you to be alone. When you write, you must post it by Friday evening's mail. I then get the letter Thursday night. The other mails are of not much use, as they are all slower than the P. and O. from Brindisi and consequently arrive about the same time. Now I must finish. Give my love to all about you, and to Mrs. Dremel and Minnie. God bless you dearest Mother.

yr. affec.
A.

P.S. You might invest in a Baedeker (he is better than Murray) and follow up what I do and where I go with greater interest.

In the following letter, Sullivan notes the unusual proper names for the donkeys he rides in Egypt. Lillie Langtry was a "society" woman who went on the stage, and a favorite of the Prince of Wales. Mrs. William Cornwallis West lived in fashionable Eaton Place. Sullivan writes about the rumors on an insurrection, which did occur later in 1882. It began with an Arab revolt, and was defeated by a British army at Tel el-Kebir. Sir John Goss was Sullivan's instructor of harmony at the Royal

Academy of Music. Sullivan loved to make fun of his closest friends, as demonstrated by his comments concerning Edward Dicey and George Grove. In the original letter, there is a notation in Dicey's hand, bracketing Sullivan's criticism of him with the word, "Impudence." Lord Granville was British Foreign Secretary; the Khedive, a nominal Egyptian ruler; Paul Gambetta, French Prime Minister. Finch was a servant of Sullivan. Sydney Dremel was the son of one of his mother's best friends. Sir Frederic Goldsmid was a British Major-General, serving as the Controller of the Daira Sanya.

Cairo, 23 Jan. 1882

Dearest Mum,

I was so glad to get your letter last Thursday forwarded by Smythe, and to know all goes well and happily. I also got letters from the girls, full of delight at their first lessons in riding. Here we ride donkeys principally, and all the donkeys have names. I often ride a capital, white donkey who is called "Prince of Wales". "Mrs. Langtry" and "Mrs. Cornwallis West" are also favourite donkeys.
Since I wrote to you last mail, I have done nothing new. It has been too cold to take excursions. We have had a fortnight of very cold weather, and as there are no fireplaces in our rooms, we sit and shiver. Yesterday and today it is much warmer, and I think the cold is over now. I hope so, otherwise we might as well be in England. It is the cold I dread always. This has been a very bad season for Cairo, so few people here comparatively speaking. They have been frightened by the rumours of insurrection, cholera, and all sorts of big fears. There has been no cholera at all, but it broke out amongst the pilgrims coming from Mecca. They were however placed in severe quarantine the other side of the Isthmus, and so its entrance was stopped. As for insurrection, there is no fear of that at present. But it is not to be denied that there are much fewer people here this season than there are generally. The great historical event of the week was my playing the organ at the English church service yesterday. Being greatly pressed to do so, I bashfully consented, so we had a choir practice of several ladies and gentlemen Saturday afternoon, and yesterday morning a very large congregation attended. Our gallant band sang very well, especially "Onward Christian Soldiers" (my tune) and the service was a marked success. But as service begins at 10:30, and I had to get up at 8:30 in consequence, I told Dean Butcher (the parson) he must not expect it again. He of course saw the "justice" of my remark.

I have been three weeks here today, and time goes dreadfully quickly. I have done nothing particular, except finish poor Sir John Goss' anthem, and I have also sketched out a few feeble ideas for other works. However, I find now from the experiments I have already made that it is useless to try and write whilst you are in the midst of new scenery, people, habits and customs, but that <u>afterwards</u> the effect is very great and one's power is redoubled and freshness restored. So I shan't bother my head about writing here, but sow the seed to be reaped when I get home again.

Dicey is very well and sends his love to you. His intellect is feeble, but he is not dangerous. He passes the greater part of his time in writing letters to important personages – Lord Granville, The Khedive, Gambetta, Rothschild etc., but of course Finch has strict orders not to post them! His appetite is good, I am glad to say. Grove is an imposter. He sends a message by Smythe every week to say he is going to write, but he doesn't write. Has he been to Egypt? I know he was in the Holy Land, but I don't think he came to Cairo. Oh if he would but come. Tell him there is nothing more Eastern than Cairo – nothing more striking. He shall have a special donkey and we will call it "G".

If this warm weather now setting in lasts, I shall go up the Nile shortly. I was strongly pressed to go today with the Masons, The Bishop and Goldsmids who have gone, but much as I should have liked their society, the weather was too cold. It is not at all warm of a night on the Nile boats. I shall wait about a fortnight probably and then go up. It is an excursion of ten days to go as far as Luxor and back. At Luxor you see Thebes and the Temple of Karnak.

I am so glad to hear that Sydney Dremel is at home and has got a commission. It will be a great comfort to his mother to have him again; and his father will be pleased that he has got a definite career. Give my love to Mrs. Dremel and to Minnie, and whilst you are distributing my love, give some of it to Charlotte and the girls. God bless you dear Mother. I hope you are comfortable and not suffering from cold. Write to me by the next mail. Friday's is the best.

yr. affec.
A.

Sullivan had not intended to stay so long in Egypt, but Dicey's business was not finished in time for them to leave before the end of March. Sullivan's ability to describe his experiences is wonderfully illustrated in the following letter. A Dervish is a member of one of the mystical religious orders of the Islamic religion. Sir Auckland Colvin was the chief British financial adviser in Egypt. Fulham is the area of greater London where Sullivan's nieces and nephews lived. *Qui Vive* in English is "in the know."

Cairo 29 Jan. 1882

Dearest Mum,

Here is the warm weather back again, I hope. We have had a long spell of cold wind, and deserve warmth.

I have not been to church, although it is Sunday, but have passed the morning in writing business letters. How I do wish letter writing were made a crime punishable by death, and telegrams reduced to five words a penny. How much happier we should all be. I have been indoors writing all the morning. It is nearly two, and I have missed much of the brilliant sunshine in consequence. I have begun this, because it is so much easier to finish a letter than to begin one. This is the most enervating place in the world, I think. If you once begin to be lazy, you can never stop, but are carried on with a mad impetus until from sheer exhaustion at doing nothing, you write a letter or read one.

I can't do any paper work here, but it doesn't matter. On Friday, I went to see the Howling Dervishes, and a pretty sight they were. I drove with the Colvins to a small mosque in the midst of a lot of ruined and half completed structures at Old Cairo. We were shown into the mosque by an attendant, sat down on chairs and looked at our friends the Dervishes. It was not a pleasant sight, or one calculated to make one say proudly, "I, too, am a man like these", but it was interesting. They stood in a circle, one boss Dervish in the middle, a sort of conductor whose motions they followed; and at one side were two or three gifted vocalists who sang real Arab music, accompanied by tom-toms. This collection of human beings then howled and gasped (breathing "Al-lah") and swayed their bodies backwards and forwards and sideways, their long hair waving in the air giving them a wild and mad appearance. They went on for 20 minutes without stopping, then a minute or two quiet whilst a verse of the Koran was read, and then off they went again. It lasted two hours, but I was only there an hour. At the end, they all quietly did up their hair and assumed their turbans and then smoked cigarettes as if nothing had happened.
These were the Howling Dervishes. Next Friday I am going to see the Dancing Dervishes. After all, it was very interesting, and not much worse than some of the performances by the Shakers in England and America. Last night, after dinner, a party of us, the Colvins, myself and one or two others drove out to the great fair at the Abbasiyeh, a bit of the desert near Cairo, and saw a most extraordinary gathering – a great collection of tents, some of enormous size, erected in a circle, all brilliantly illuminated, and each containing the representations of some sect, or the sheik of a district or guild. In every tent there were a number of worshipers. In some, they were reciting the Koran, in others, howling like the Dervishes; indeed in one big tent there was a circle of a hundred howlers, all swaying their bodies and prostrating themselves. One tent contained a devotee who was dancing exactly like the figure the children have got at Fulham. Then there was a tremendous procession of about a couple of thousand men carrying torches and candles, playing pipes, beating drums and singing in the most hideous fashion; the Sheiks walking gravely in the middle. They walked round the circle twice, and then stood in front of a large and splendid tent wherein sat a chief eunuch who was a "hadji" or sacred man, because he had been to Mecca, and also two important Sheiks. They chanted something in honour of these "prominent citizens", as the American would say, and then retired. The whole scene was one of the most striking things I ever saw. The tents,

the lights, the singing, howling, dancing, and this wild looking Arab gathering all throwing such fervour into their religious exercises, took me into another world, far away from European civilization.

I must explain to you that this fair is held every year at this time, and is preparatory to the great ceremony of the Moulid or bringing back of the sacred carpet from Mecca by the pilgrims. The carpet is brought into the town in great state on a camel, and the pilgrims disperse. The "Doséh," which used to be the important and exciting part of the ceremony was suppressed last year, and so I suppose we shan't have it this year. It must have been a horrible sight. The Sheik of the Sahadiyeh dervishes mounted on horseback rides across the prostrate bodies of the fanatics, who by hundreds throw themselves on to the ground, closely wedged together making a human road. I believe the carpet is to be brought in next Thursday, so we are on the qui vive of course. Tell Grove that the Boulak Museum, being so close to me, of course I have not yet been, as every afternoon I make a resolve to go in. But I am going with a couple of fellows on Wednesday to meet Brugseh the director who will show us everything to advantage. The mummy of Pharaoh's daughter who picked up Moses is there. There are no fresh arrivals here, except a party of "personally conducted" who have gone up the Nile. It is a bad season as far as trade etc. goes, but it is pleasanter for us who are here. I don't know how long a stay, or when I go, or where I go, and I don't much care. That is a happy state of existence I have looked forward to for years, but never experienced 'till now.

I am pretty well in health, but am confined to one pair of shoes, as I have a sore heel. God bless you. My love to all.

yr. affec.
A.

Sullivan tells of his increased interest in Arab music, and describes the dancing dervishes. Sir Edward Malet was a British consul in Egypt. Eduard Eugene Dulier was a colonel in the Egyptian army. The "young Princes" are Prince Albert Victor and Prince George, sons of the Prince of Wales. They were serving on the HMS Bacchante. Henry Peveril Le Mesurier was president of the Egyptian Railway Administration. The "new piece" Sullivan was starting to write was the first act of *Iolanthe*.

Cairo Sunday 26 Feb. 1882

Dearest Mum,

O Lord another week has flown. As the hymn says, "flown as quickly as a dream", and I have no incidents of stirring interest to relate. The beginning of this week was gorgeously hot and we thought the cold had vanished for the rest of the year, but no, on Thursday there was a change, and it blew a regular gale all day and all night, and ever since it has been cold and dull. Today it is warm again and so I shall go for a walk this afternoon.

In the absence of any news, I will just take my diary and see what I have done this week. Monday, after I had dispatched all my letters, I sat on the terrace here, still feeling very seedy, but after a time I put on strength and rose as one man, dressed myself and went to dine at the Fitzgeralds. A pleasant dinner, and a lot of folks after dinner. Later on I went to Tigrane Bey's again, who had arranged a repetition of the Arab musical soiree that I described to you when I first came here. It was exactly the same as before. But this time I was much more knowing about it, having had my ears acclimatized to the Arab music; and I enjoyed it even more than the first time. The musicians themselves were delighted to see me. We exchanged salaams, shook hands, and said "Neharak Said" (Thy day be happy) and "E zeyyak" (How is your health?) etc. Drank coffee, smoked cigarettes, and parted with much regret at 1:45. I again tried my old friend the "Nei" or flute, and in five minutes succeeded in not being able to elicit a single sound from the instrument. Tuesday we had a touch of the "Hamseen" or warm desert wind, which brings clouds of dust. In the evening, I dined at the VanderNests (Belgian Consul). [...] After dinner a lot of people came in and the young folks danced until 2 a.m. I played "hap" with the elders, except when I was called upon to play "Sir Roger de Coverly".

Wednesday being Ash Wednesday, I had eggs for breakfast (like your grandmother), having had nothing else since I arrived here. I then did a little shopping and got two or three lovely old pieces of stuff. In the evening Mrs. Mason had a small gathering to tea in their rooms. […] Being ostensibly a quiet party, we made more row than usual, especially over a game called "grab" which I daresay the children know. Thursday was cold and windy. I was seedy again, and didn't do much, but went to another "quiet" party at the Le Mesuriers. He is head of the railways. Coming home my hat was blown off (I told you I had no exciting incidents) and I chased it earnestly and steadily for some time, and caught it before it reached the desert.

Friday, I went to see the dancing dervishes. Their dancing consists in twirling slowly and steadily like humming tops; and as they have long petticoats, they look like the cheeses you used to make for us when we were boys. After they had danced a long time, they all knelt down, and the Sheik recited a prayer. Then they bowed and touched the ground with their foreheads, and the ceremony was over. It was much more devotional than the "howlers". They were very grave and very dignified.

Afterwards I went to see two or three mosques. One of them, near the Gama-el Ghuri being especially striking from the lovely blue tiles with which one side is covered. From there I went to see something more modern, viz: Prince Henry of Prussia, who had just arrived from his trip up the Nile. I drove down to the river and found him on his Dahabieh (Nile boat) arranging his packages for departure to Alexandria the next morning. He was so glad to see me and expressed such surprise and delight that it gave me enormous pleasure. I stayed a long time with him, and then left. He was traveling incognito as "Comte de Berg". At night, there was a party at the Moneys. Money is an official here, draws 3000 pounds a year for keeping the key of one of the cash boxes.

Yesterday afternoon I went shopping again, and bought some pretty stuff to cover the drawing room furniture with. In the evening dined with the Duliers. […] They are very well off, and are very nice people. Tonight I dine with Malet, our minister here. Now, of course, this is all very stupid, but I have nothing else to say. I can't make exciting incidents. We shall have a little more next week perhaps – viz: the arrival of the young Princes. They are to be here about Thursday and will stay two or three days before they go up the Nile. […] I expect it will be blazing hot up in the Soudan [sp.], because, of course, the further south one goes the hotter it gets, and there is nothing but desert and dust except just along the line of the Nile, vegetation springing from its overflow.

I employ my mornings in sketching at the new piece to follow "Patience", Gilbert having sent me the lst Act complete. I was obliged to give up the Bach Society's motets, as I had to get it done by a certain date. It was impossible as I lost a fortnight, owing to a series of bad headaches I had. Bile, liver and weather combined to make me miserable for some days. My treasure of a servant that I brought with me (Finch) is a failure. He is not a good servant – lazy, lightheaded, and worst of all a tendency to drink. This last is quite enough, so we part when we touch English soil again. – Oh the bother of servants; and I shall have to get a cook also, besides a man. It is enough to make me marry, but the cure would be more awful than the disease. I can get rid of servants, but not of a wife, especially as she is my wife.

Tell Grove to ease his mind, that I know the Boulac Museum by heart almost, and that there is nothing I haven't seen in it. If he hasn't seen it, no description will give him an idea of some of the colour and workmanship which are perhaps ten, twenty, thirty thousand years old. I don't know whether he has been to Cairo or not. I suppose he was here when he made his journey to the Holy Land. Now goodbye. God bless you all.

yr. affec.
A.

Sullivan and Dicey left Egypt, and continued their travels in Italy. Sullivan's "Herculamente" is actually "Herculaneum," and he corrects this in the next letter. When the volcano Mount Vesuvius erupted in 769AD it engulfed the two flourishing towns of Pompeii and Herculaneum. Sullivan kept in contact with his former teacher, the Rev. Thomas Helmore.

Hotel des Etrangers
April 1, 1882
Naples

Dearest Mum,

Here we are, alive and well after a beastly passage in a small, dirty, rolling tub of a boat – uncomfortable, slow and the cooking worse than poison. We couldn't get a big steamer from Port Said on Sunday, as there wasn't one, so we stayed in Cairo 'till Monday. Left amidst the regrets of a crowd of friends who accompanied us to the station, slept at Alexandria, and left the next morning early in the Messageries Maritimes boat called "Tage". We arrived here this evening in a pelting shower. Vesuvius smoking, and looking very gloomy and angry in the black thunder clouds which surrounded it, and after an hour and a half's delay at the custom house, where every single thing we had was opened, and which tried our tempers sorely, we came to this most comfortable hotel overlooking the Bay. Sarah Bernhardt left this morning, and I have her rooms! They are gorgeous, and I think must have been done up expressly for her. Mirrors and blue velvet in the sitting room and beautiful white muslin linings on the walls of the bedroom, covered with bunches of artificial white flowers. I have no doubt I shall look lovely in bed tonight. After dinner (which was a god-like feast, after what we have endured the last five days) we went to the San Carlo, and saw half of a feeble opera by Mercadante, and a splendid ballet. But what a theatre it is! Magnificent, and the largest in the world. I am very glad I have seen it. We also drove about the town a bit. Tomorrow we are going to Sorrento where the Masons are staying. – Monday to Pompeii, Herculamente, and on Tuesday we go off to Rome. It is Holy Week and I want to try and hear the celebrated "Miserere" of Allegri in the Sistine Chapel. I may stay in Rome two, three or four days, but I shall be in Paris on Monday the 10th at the latest, and then to get home will be very short work. If you think this will be a long letter, you are mistaken for it is three o'clock a.m. and I am going to bed. But I must take it downstairs to the porter, as the post leaves at 7 in the morning. I shall send you a telegram in the morning, and hope you will get it, but doubt Italian intelligence.

God bless you. My love to all. Give my love to Mr. and Mrs. Helmore. Tell him I wish he were in Rome with me next week. We should enjoy the Sistine Chapel together immensely.

yr. affec.
A.

One of the last letters of this trip was written from Rome on his way home to England. As he wrote this letter, he had no idea that it would be among the last letters he would write to his mother. A month after he returned to England, Mary Clementina Sullivan died. Sullivan's many letters to his mother tell us more of this multi-faceted man. They represent the desire of a devoted son to try to give his mother the opportunity of vicariously "living through" many of his most special experiences. The phrase "the Pope has chosen (or been compelled by the Cardinals) to consider himself a prisoner" referred to the hostile anti-Catholic climate in Italy due to Pope Leo XIII's continuing the unpopular policies of Pius IX towards Italy without major modifications.

Hotel Bristol. Rome
8 April, 1882

Dearest Mum,

I am just leaving here – Proud Rome – and by the time you get this I shall be in Paris. I leave at 2 this afternoon and travel right on, through the Mont Cenis, without changing, and hope to arrive in Paris Monday morning at 5:15 – a pretty long journey.

I have been too much occupied in sightseeing to write to you since my letter from Naples. I spent 3 days at Naples, visiting Mount Vesuvius on Sunday, and Pompeii on Monday. To Vesuvius we drove through

Torre del Greco, Portici, Herculaneum and up the mountain 'till we arrived at the foot of the cone. There we got into a car and were pulled up by a traction engine. It looks perfectly dreadful before you ascend, as it is almost a perpendicular ascent. We got to the top, and then walked over burning stones, lava, cinders etc., amidst the most noxious sulphur vapours, to the edge of the crater. There was a great rumbling going on inside, and every minute an angry roll of thunder, and a shower of fire, smoke, and cinders came bursting out. I went a little way down, but not far, as it was so unpleasant. There was something very mysterious and awestriking in the scene. It was night when we left, and we had a most magnificent view returning in the moonlight; Vesuvius throwing out angry red flames and smoke, and below us Naples and the little towns about it, all spread out around the bay, looking like a circlet of gold. The next day we went to Pompeii, and that I shall not attempt to describe. It is more impressive and wonderful than I thought. Whilst at Naples, I went to the S. Carlo Theatre – the finest and largest in the world. Tuesday we left, and arrived here at night. I thought, being Holy Week, there would be grand nights and impressive music, but I am doomed to disappointment. Since the Pope has chosen (or been compelled by the Cardinals) to consider himself a prisoner, all the grand functions have ceased. I have heard inferior music in St. Peter's and St. John Lateran, but it was very inferior. St. Peter's itself is grandly impressive. I stayed a long time looking at it. Although it is colossal in size, its splendidly balanced proportions prevent it from looking over big. Coutts Lindsay is here. We went out for a long drive together yesterday, and I dined with him at night. On Thursday I dined with the Storys. Story is a sculptor and poet, celebrated as you know. I have had a birds eye of everything – just seen the outside. I should like to come and spend a winter here, but at the present moment, I am more anxious to get home, as I am getting rather homesick. You will see me the end of next week I hope.

Love to all. God bless you

yr. affec.
A.

Sullivan returned home, which allowed him to spend the next six weeks near his mother. In mid-May, Clementina Sullivan became very ill, passing away on May 27th. A portion of Sullivan's diary entry read,

"I rushed upstairs, and was alone in the room – alone, that is, with dear Mother's lifeless body – her soul had gone to God."

Chapter Six

"Stick together, one for all..."

(Taking Care of Family)

Charlotte's new husband, Benjamin Hutchinson, continued to have difficulty finding a job in England. Charlotte's brother, William Lacy, who lived in Los Angeles, told Charlotte and Ben of the great potential in Southern California and urged them to join him with their family. They decided (in spite of Sullivan's discouragement) to make the move. The family left London in December 1883 to sail to New York from Liverpool, and then by train to Los Angeles. Another family tragedy occurred a year later. In January 1885, about two months after Charlotte had given birth to her last child, Harold, Charlotte died. Sullivan was now almost completely supporting the family. He wrote to the children the following:

1 Queen's Mansions
Victoria Street S.W.
Saturday, 31 Jan: 1885

My dearest children,

You are suffering from the greatest loss and the greatest grief that can arrive to you in the whole of your lives, and my heart is full of sympathy for you – no words of mine can assuage the first bitter pain which such a loss as yours causes you. But there is one reflection which when you are calmer, will be a blessed consolation to you, and that is your mother loved you dearly, and that she also knew & appreciated your great love for her. She was devoted to you, & you returned her devotion & tenderness in an unmistakable manner. This will always be a comfort to you, & will take away all bitterness from the regret which must last all your lives – and now, in your prayers, night & morning, pray that your dear mother may have joined your father in God's eternal Rest, and that you all may lead such lives on earth, that hereafter you may be taken to where our hope is they are. Don't let the active demonstration of your love for her cease now that she is gone, but continue it by doing such things as you know she would wish you to do, and by never doing that which you would be ashamed for her to see. Above all things, my dear ones, be united. Stick together, one for all – all for one – bickerings & quarrelling's amongst brothers and sisters are unworthy, unnecessary, & injurious. In the battle of life you want all your strength & all your devotion to each other. Therefore cling to each other with unyielding tenacity, & let nothing break the bond. In me you know you have a second father, and your best friend.

God bless & comfort you all.
Your loving uncle
Arthur Sullivan

Sullivan decided he must make the trip to America's far west to visit and assist his young family. He was in the midst of writing *The Mikado*, so couldn't leave England immediately. He also knew that William Lacy and his wife lived very near to the young family, and could help them with any immediate needs (Amy was now 22, and the next eldest, Florence, was 19). He began his trip on June 20th. 1885. The trip took him away from London for more than four months. After a challenging trip across the United States, he arrived in Los Angeles in late July. He arranged for a housekeeper to live with the young family, as well as a man to serve as a gardener and, in Sullivan's words, "general factotum". He, of course, paid for all of this as well as continuing his regular financial allotments. He

later made full payment for their house. He left Los Angeles on August 29th, and headed for New York City where *The Mikado* was being produced. He sailed from New York on October 14th, 1885. The comic opera he refers to is *Ruddigore*. "Dick" refers to Sullivan's nephew. Louis was Sullivan's manservant. "Cissie" was the family nickname for Maud.

Yorktown
Fambro Station
Saturday
22 May

Dearest Cissie,

I write to you, firstly, because I owe you a letter, and secondly because you have just been confirmed, and I am very pleased that you have been. Who confirmed you? Was it a Bishop of the American Episcopal Church? Write & tell me all about it. I also want to know how the domestic affairs are getting on – how the garden looks – what is growing – what has grown already & how it is laid out – send me a groundplan of all the ground next time, showing how every part is apportioned. Dick can draw that. Have you got the new well yet, or any other supply of water? Let me know all details – what became of Rose after she left you, & is Ruth happy or unhappy? I am down at this little village hard at work writing for the Leeds Festival. The village is where your father and I were brought up as children, when grandpapa was at the Royal Military College. And oddly enough my lodgings are right next door to our old house, and as it belongs also to my landlord, and there is a communication between the two houses, I may be said to be living in the very house where we lived so long, many years ago. Isn't it strange? I can't do any writing in London, I am so dreadfully interrupted and disturbed, and I have much to do – "The Golden Legend" for the Leeds Festival, the entire organization for the Festival (no finale work), a new comic opera, directly the Leeds work is finished, to produce in October. Then I had to do the Ode for the opening of the exhibition, which the Prince of Wales begged me to set – so you see my hands are pretty full. Now I have received a great privilege at the hands of Mr. Mackay (Bonanza Mackay). He has given me the permission (and a book of telegraph forms!) to telegraph to Los Angeles every Sunday free of charge, and has arranged for you children to do the same over to me! Now isn't that splendid? I daresay before you receive this you will have got full instructions – book of forms etc. about the privilege, the messages and the forms from me to Amy, and vice versa. Mr. Mackay explained to me that Sunday was an idle day comparatively speaking for the cable (it is the Commercial Cable Company) and that if I sent my messages up to the office in London on Saturday or Sunday, they would always be sent free of charge on the Sunday. Of course we mustn't abuse this kindness on his part, by sending inordinately long or foolish messages, but we can every Sunday have a little interchange as to health etc. Bertie is very well and complains bitterly that you hardly ever write to him. Why don't you? Now I must finish. I got your joint birthday card this morning. Although late, it is very welcome. Give my love to all. I will write to Amy and Florry shortly, but it is so difficult to get time to write a letter, after I have been writing music all day long. God bless you all,

yr. affect. uncle

Arthur

I am sending Louis up to town to post this, otherwise it won't go by today's mail – the return ticket 2nd class is 6/9. You can owe it to me!

There is a wide gap in the letter dates between the last letter and the next one. During this gap in time Sullivan wrote some of his most memorable works, *Ruddigore* (1887), *The Yeomen of the Guard* (1888), *The Gondoliers* (1889), and *Ivanhoe* (1891). This letter is written to Sullivan's brother-in-law, William Lacy, who lived very close to the children, and kept in contact with Sullivan about them. Sullivan's old illness which he describes as the "usual" pain had strongly reasserted itself. Maud (Cissie) and Amy had developed strong differences. Charles Stephens was married to Amy's sister, Florence, until she died in 1891. In 1893 Charles married Amy. It is interesting that Maud often stayed at the home of William Lacy; and thus it is not surprising that in 1893, Maud married

William's second son, Richard.

Saturday, July 18, 1891

My dear William,

I can't frame any stereotyped excuse for not writing to you before. The only reason I can give – the true one – is that I have been so horribly depressed these past few months, that all my energy & strength have been take out of me. Over and over again, I have said "today I will write to William", and then comes that awful lack of the power of beginning anything.

I stick in my chair, and read to the very last line of the advertisements in the *Times* because I haven't the moral strength to set about doing what I propose to do. The fact is I suppose, that I have overworked myself these last three years – every day for three years my imagination has had to be called into play. Every day, I have had to invent something; & this year after the production of "Ivanhoe" the reaction came, and I regularly broke down. The smallest incident in daily life became an event, and to write a letter seemed to me a task too great for my strength – it required a great effort. And that is the reason and the only one that I have not written to you before. Please don't be hard upon me, I daresay you know yourself the difficulty of arousing yourself into action of any kind, when these morbid fits come over one.

Now I am troubled with my old complaint (kidneys) and tomorrow morning I start for Coutrexeville (in the Vosges) for a month's cure at the water there, and please God shall come back strong and well. Again I feel I can't leave England again without writing to you, and hence this letter.

These disputes between Amy and Maud are really very vexing and I am thoroughly disappointed, and besides being vexing they are likely to lead to awkward results. Each of them writes to me and gives me her version. Amy says Maud is uncontrollable and hates the quiet life upon the hill. Maud says she can't stand Mr. Stephens and that he is constantly there. Now of course these are idle trifles, and there must be something more to cause a breakup of the household – a breakup which is most unfortunate, and which I resent very much....Maud kicks I know, and always did against any sisterly or even motherly control, and naturally enough, likes society and the world. There is no harm in this, but in order to indulge more freely in it, she has no right to take her own independent way, until she has earned her independence. My difficulty now is how I shall manage so that no injustice shall be done to any one of the children, and at the same time protect myself.

I confess it grieves me to think that the home should be broken up, & after so much money has been spent upon it, that it should be left for a mere nothing. I have always hoped that the property would very much improve and increase in value, and that I could sell it, house, furniture and all for a good round sum, and then settle this sum on the children individually, so that they could be independent. But Amy seems to imply that the property on the hill does not increase in value, as it is so far from the tramway, in spite of the railway being so near. If this is the case, it is very disheartening, and you must feel it also, as I know you had a good deal of ground up there.

I wish my dear William, you would advise me in the matter – advise me whether it could be sold, & how much one ought to expect for it. God knows I don't begrudge the money I give the children, but I am sure you can realize what an anxiety it is for me, and also what a pull it is upon me to find $3000 a year for them, and to bring them up with the idea that this is always to go on. And now Maud of course chafes at being beholden to Amy for whatever money she requires, and would like I have no doubt (and very naturally) her separate income. But so long as Amy has the house to keep going and all the other children with her, I can hardly reduce her income because she and Maud don't get on together. If the house could be sold, I would divide the income, and let them live in the town, where they liked best, allowing Amy so much for each child under age that lived with her. This is the only plan feasible that I can see, which would satisfy all of them. It depends however upon what you say, and what you advise. You are on the spot – you have the children's interest at heart as much as I have – and you know best how things ought to shape out. Therefore don't treat me as badly as I have treated you, but write and give me the benefit of your advice. I shall be very grateful for it I assure you.

Bertie is getting on very well, I heard from him yesterday from Paramaribo on the coast of Dutch Guiana. He is with the French Cable Company laying cables. He is a great favourite with his chief (Seaton the engineer) and seems to have settled down to the hard work of life with earnestness. He expects to be home in August some time.

Now I will close for today – having once made the effort to write a coherent letter, it won't be so hard for me to do it again! I hope your own affairs are prospering, for you ought to be as rich as you are generous and kind to others. Give my love to all of them, boys and girls. Use all or any parts of this letter you think desirable, in conferring with Amy and Maud. Amy in her last letter gives a much better account of Dick, and says he is quiet and steady, and she thinks he is turning over a new leaf. I hope it is so.

Goodbye, old man, God bless you.

yr. affect.

Arthur Sullivan

Sullivan gave additional financial help when his nieces and nephews married. As previously mentioned, Maud married Richard Lacy, second eldest son of William Lacy. They were first cousins (Our family loves to say, "Oh that's what's wrong with all of us!"). The letter gives fatherly advice as to Maud's relationship with Amy, her elder sister. Loughborough is not far north of Leicester.

1 Queen's Mansions
Victoria Street S.W.
22 Oct: 1892

My dearest Maud,

I wired you after I received your letter, & now write to say that as your Uncle William approves of your marriage with his son, I of course gladly give my assent also. My recollection of Dick Lacy is a pleasant one. I always thought him a nice boy, so I hope you will be very happy, and try to adapt yourselves to each other's tastes, & be lenient to each other's little failings, if either of you have any.

According to my promise when I was in Los Angeles, I will give you 500 pounds the day you are married, settled of course on yourself, so that you may not go empty handed to your husband. Let me know when the happy day is to be.

And now that you are going to have a house of your own, can you manage to get on better with Amy? All these quarrelling's and bickerings between children who have neither father nor mother are deplorable & discouraging, and could easily be avoided in a little giving & taking equally. You ought never to have left the home, & that is why I wouldn't make you a separate allowance. Now there is not more reason for dispute, & so I hope the next letter I get from you will tell me that all is forgotten, & that peace & affection reign once more.

Bertie is staying here (from Saturday to Monday) having run up from his work at Loughborough, & sends his love & a blessing. God bless you my dear child.

yr. affec. uncle
A.S.

Sullivan wrote to Bertie from St. Moritz in Switzerland (the location of famous mineral baths) in 1896, the same year as *The Grand Duke*. Sullivan was now 54, four years before his death. Clotilde Racquet was Sullivan's housekeeper from 1885 until he died. Wilfred Bendall became his secretary

(following Smythe), but, being a composer, could also help Sullivan with musical concerns. Adolph Hirsch was a friend of Sullivan. Blankenbergh is on the Belgian coast. The following disciplinary letter must have been a difficult one for Sullivan to write.

Saturday, 22 Aug. 1896
St. Moritz

Dear Bertie,

Acting on your admirable suggestion, I haven't written much to you, as I knew Clotilde would share my news with you. There has not been much news to share, for here "one day resembleth another" except in the matter of weather, and there is a delirious dullness in the life generally. I get up in the morning (before I go out even), breakfast, read the *Times* and *Telegraph*, and then stroll about 'till lunch time if it doesn't pour. Out again from lunch to dinner time, if it doesn't pour. Then the regular Swiss hotel evening, sitting in the large hall, smoking, talking, and passing the time until we come up into my sitting room for an hours chat before going to bed. When it rains, it does so conscientiously – never ceasing even for meals. The first three days (Sunday, Mon. Tues.) of this week were divine. The sun shone brilliantly and gave warmth, whilst there was a crystal sort of coldness in the air which made one feel 21 again, and ready to walk up to the top of the Adler-Spitze before breakfast.

I don't want to come back to England yet, and shall not go back to Walton in any case, and this brings me to a matter upon which, my dear boy, I must talk to you seriously. The River House is lovely, and the place suits me admirably, but I have not had the enjoyment out of it that I looked forward to. One of the great pleasures of a place like that is to ask one's friends to stay a day or two, or even to dine and sleep only. But I have observed that although I let you stay the whole summer or autumn with me, and use the house as if it were your own, you have degrees of courtesy and welcome for my friends. If <u>you</u> like them, well and good. If not, you show it in too marked a manner to please me. I need not indicate in more detailed manner what or whom I mean, because your intelligence renders it unnecessary. But I have noticed it ever since I took the house and <u>I don't like it</u>. And the same thing I am sorry to say applies to others in the house. Their likes and dislikes are shown too plainly in the manner my guests are treated and served. I am not speaking so much of the past three months because the circumstances were exceptional, but it has always been so. Consequently, you will not be surprised that I wish so much to get rid of River House, and that I don't mean to return to it. I learn from Clotilde's letter that Mr. Bendall was very rudely treated by her and by you too. He certainly did not complain, as you will see by the cutting from his letter I enclose. But <u>I</u> resent it. I gave him a pressing invitation to go down when he liked and he has never yet gone down without proposing himself beforehand. When you received his letter (I learn all this from Clotilde) and told Clotilde, which you probably forgot to do, she should have wired saying that it was not convenient for various domestic reasons and asking him to change the day of his visit. If he was <u>not</u> put off he should have been made welcome. I have long noticed that you appear anything but friendly to Bendall. I suppose it is because he attends to all my business with the greatest devotion and regularity, and you can't when I entrust anything to you. When I left, Adolph authorized you to get any calls that might be made in my absence paid at his office. You got <u>one</u> paid (Claridge's) and wired the fact to me, and that seems to have exhausted your energy, for the next one that came (Riverside Orange Co.) you returned to Bendall, after keeping it a week, without a word, and so he sent it on to me. [...] I know you would not willingly neglect anything which I asked you to do, but, my dear boy, forgetfulness and thoughtlessness are not cardinal virtues are they? With regard to Bendall, he is an old friend of mine. <u>I</u> advised him in 1869 to go to Leipzig and pursue his musical studies, and have often given him a lift since, and liked him, and although he may not possess the fascinating geniality and magnetic attraction of poor Smythe (!) yet he is a thoroughly good fellow, devoted to me, and of an aid to me such as I never hoped to obtain. Now I have liberated my soul and shall not refer to these matters again. We will both forget them.

It is still raining and no sign of its clearing up. If it continues, I shall probably leave here on Monday, and go where it is not quite so cold and damp. I will wire you where a letter will find me next. I have just telegraphed you not to write here any more. No one has bought the house yet I suppose, and neither you nor Clotilde have earned your commission.

I read in the papers here, that a most striking looking, professional beauty had been seen bathing at Blankenbergh and all that was known of her was that her clothes (which someone peeped at in the bathing machine) were marked C.R.

Now goodbye. My love to Clotilde and to all the "family".

yr. affec. Uncle
A.

The relationship between Sullivan and Mary Frances "Fanny" Ronalds was complicated, yet they remained dear friends until the end of Sullivan's life. He willed the original manuscript of *The Lost Chord* to her, and when Fanny died (several years after Sullivan) a copy of the original manuscript was buried with her. "No. 7" refers to Fanny's address. Sullivan's name for her, particularly when he communicated with Bertie, was "Auntie." The ballet was to be called *Victoria and Merrie England.* Alfred Moul was the manager of the Alhambra Theatre in Leicester Square. This theatre made a specialty of ballet.

Villa Mathilde
30 Dec. 1896
St. Jean – Villafranche
Alpes

My dear Bertie,

I didn't write to you for Christmas Day, as I knew you were at Crabbé and didn't know his address, and a Xmas day letter received two days afterwards is rather stale. So I hope this will reach you on New Year's Day and bring with it my blessing and most fervent wishes for a happy, peaceful and prosperous New Year. I think we all touched the bottom of misfortune and unhappiness this past year, and now we have hope before us, and I believe that everything <u>must</u> be better in the forthcoming year, and so, my dear boy, I hope we shall both have our part in this happiness and prosperity. I am so glad you have been a good deal to no. 7 and that you are in constant "rapport" by telephone and otherwise. Auntie took me aside at the station and entreated me to ask you to be kind and gentle to her. I told her it was not to be wondered at, if you were hard with her, considering all the trouble and unhappiness she had caused, but that if all that was over, I was sure she would find no more loving or sympathetic helping friend than you, and so I want you to be a friend and guide to her. You see, my dear Bertie, it is a very trying period of life for her. In '62 when I first knew her, all London ran after her. Later in '68, when I was there, all Paris from the Emperor downwards was at her feet, and in spite of misfortune, imprudence and jealousy, she kept this influence for many years. Now the years will tell, although her mind and spirits remain young, and this is a terrible time for any woman to go through. And so all of us who are really fond of her must be gentle and considerate.

I am working hard and successfully at my ballet, and am sending off a long scene to Moul tomorrow. Bendall is copying it, and filling in the accompt. where he is wonderfully useful. Fancy poor old Smythe filling in a harmonized accompt.!! I don't go much to Monte Carlo, because having no money to play with, there is nothing to do. [...]

I must finish or shall miss the post. It is a divine day, but my hand is cold, and I am writing directly after lunch, which makes my handwriting rather shaky and drunken looking. Clotilde has just had a beautiful new dress made which <u>fits</u>, and so she is quite happy. She tells me she has written to you. Louis said he never had such a nice letter in his life as you wrote to him. So we are all contented. God bless you.

your affect. A.S.

Sullivan expresses fatherly concerns for Bertie's health and living situation. Buxton Browne was one of Sullivan's doctors. William Matthews was a barrister friend.

Tuesday

Dear Bertie,

I am very sorry indeed to get such bad accounts of your health from Bendall and others. If you could only once get your blood into thoroughly wholesome and clean condition I feel sure you wouldn't be bothered with these constantly recurring attacks. I mean that your body would be strong enough to resist cold etc. In the meantime all you can do is to follow B. Browne's regime and do what he tells you. Had you been here the last three weeks in search of warmth and sunshine, you would have been greatly disappointed. It is exactly a fortnight today since the rain and bad weather began, and it still goes on. Yesterday we had a short spell of sunshine and so Clotilde and I took advantage of it to go over to Nice and do some shopping. The result was that we were caught in a hailstorm in the Avenue de la Gare, and did our shopping in miserable rain, arriving home at 7 in pouring rain! Oh the Sunny South.

The weather is so bad that I hardly ever go outside the house, which has the advantage of making me stick to my work. I have done all the ballet except the last scene which I haven't received from Moul yet, and have begun the scoring. As soon as the weather here has settled down fine (if it ever does) and you can scrape a first class fare together, you might run down here for a few days and recoup in health. But at present it would be folly as you couldn't go out. [...] Have you got rid of your rooms yet?
In any case I hope you have given notice, as it is a heavy drag upon you. I should think you could find a comfortable room near the Garrick, costing very little and by means of the Club, live cheaply – like Willie Matthews used to do. The rent you pay now is killing. We are very comfortable and contented here. We play Duratzki [?] every night, and I lose steadily. I never saw anything like the cards Clotilde holds. I have only been twice inside the Casino during the last four weeks, so I don't ruin myself there!

There is a heavy storm coming on again – the sky is getting black as ink. God bless you. I hope you can give me a better account of your health next time you write. Tell Auntie I was much pleased with her letter and good wishes, and will write to her soon

yr. affect. A.

Eight months later Sullivan wrote from Splügen, Switzerland, where he was getting treatment at a health spa. Sullivan's fatherly advice and encouragement to Bertie continued. Bertie had found an occupation as a stockbroker in London.

Hotel Bodenhaus
Splügen
Saturday, 28th. Aug. 1897

Dear Bertie,

We have just arrived here (6p.m.) after a most heavenly drive from Thusis, and, as we are a long way from the centre of civilization, where you are, I write this at once, so that it may reach you on the eventful day – your birthday. God bless you, and give you many years of happiness and prosperity.

You are nearly thirty – half way through the average of man's life; and so, my dear boy, leave being a boy (as you are in many respects) and assume all the qualities and attributes and responsibilities of manhood.

Clotilde says you have had a good time in the City lately. I am delighted to hear it, and hope it may continue, not as a flash in the pan, but steadily and continuously. Build up your business in such a way that you can always count upon a good average income, and then spend always less than you earn.
Sunday morning. I was interrupted last night, and so finish this now. I shall post it here, so that you get it Tuesday morning I hope.

A telegram forwarded from Thusis came last night from Clotilde. I thought I had my code in my bag, but Louis had taken it out, and left it on my table at Thusis, so I cannot decipher it. I hope it is nothing of great importance.
Just after we got here last evening the clouds came over the mountains and it began to rain. Then it poured all night, and all this morning, so we could not make our little walking excursions as we hoped to do. It seems clearing up now (11.30 a.m.) and looks hopeful, so I trust we shall have a dry drive back to Thusis. How magnificent the road from Thusis to here is! I have done it three or four times now, but it is always new and delightful to me. Louis is in a great state of excitement, and points out every spot where a battle has taken place, or some great event happened. But his interest in life doesn't extend much beyond the Huns and Hannibal and the Middle Ages – except Napoleon. He is dead nuts on him. I was amused with Clotilde's account of your bicycle trip. It must have been great fun, and it is really astonishing how she manages to carry through everything she undertakes. I will never jeer at her bâtons anymore. Hooray! The rain has cleared off, and the sun has come out; so we shall have a lovely journey back.

No more today. God bless you. Give my love to Clotilde.

yr. affect. uncle
A.

A year later, 1898, the same year as *The Beauty Stone*, and two years before his death, Sullivan continued to help his nieces and nephews. His nephew, George Sullivan, had asked for Sullivan's financial help while in the Yukon in Canada, very near Alaska, during the gold rush. George was in Canada perhaps with his younger brother, William. Lord Rosebery was Prime Minister of the United Kingdom from March 1894 to June 1895. Mr. and Mrs. Paul Hardy were friends of Sullivan. Sullivan writes from Austria.

Badeschloss
Bad-Gastein
Monday, July 25, 1898

Dear Bertie,

I have been waiting all the week for your letter about the boys' money, and I am glad to say it came this morning. I was naturally anxious to know whether it had been cabled or posted, and what chances it had of reaching them soon. It will doubtless come in very useful to the poor boys, who are probably not killing themselves with luxurious eating and drinking. Amy also will be in receipt of my letter about now and will write and tell the boys to expect to hear from me. I should think there was business to be done up in those parts (beginning in a small way) in banking, that is the cashing of drafts – giving drafts in exchange for gold, and general agency.

Two intelligent, energetic, upright young fellows ought to be able to do it as well as, and indeed better than a company with a high sounding title and a body of ravenous shareholders. That's the way fortunes have been made in California and Nevada in the old days and this newly worked district bears about the same relationship to civilization that Calif.[ornia] did in those days. If I were 25 years younger, out I'd go. A good store and agency is better and surer than prospecting. I have begun a letter to George and will finish it this week expounding my views on things in general.

Yes, things are not lively here, but I am well contented, as the air is magnificent; is doing me much good, and I am never dull when alone. I have had a companion the last three days – Lord Rosebery, and we have taken our walks together. He is a most interesting man and brilliantly clever. Poor Mrs. Paul Hardy and her girls arrived last night. I say "poor" because she was treated even much worse than I was. Her rooms were ordered a month ago – every detail given, and the landlord wrote back to say that everything she wanted should be ready for her – rooms on the 2nd floor (or 1st) looking south etc. etc. When she arrived it was the old story. Instead of good rooms on the 1st or 2nd, there were two pokey cupboards on the ground floor next to the water and very damp, and the landlord half drunk and very insolent. I have

managed to get her something here to begin with, and in a day or two my landlord will be able to let her have a nice apartment. The scoundrel at the other place now wants her to pay a week's rent, and two days over the week as well! If she can manage to get her luggage away without a row, I have advised her not to pay anything.
Give my love to Clotilde and tell her she will get a letter from me (in answer to the <u>many</u> <u>nice</u> <u>long</u> ones she has written me) the day after you receive this. [...] Louis was much pleased at your remembrance of him.

Ever your affect. uncle, A.

Sullivan's strong concern for the health of Bertie and "Auntie" continues.

Tirolerhof
Innsbruck
Monday, Aug. 8th. 1898

My dear Bertie,

Clotilde's telegram saying you were in B.B's hospital gave me a shock. After your letter, received that morning, it was unexpected. I shan't know any details until I get to Thusis tomorrow evening, but I presume from Clotilde's telegram yesterday that you are going on all right, whatever may have occurred. I wish both you and she wouldn't be so sparing of telegrams when illness is about when I am a long way from home. I am naturally uneasy, and a few telegrams don't cost so much as the anxiety I feel. You are at liberty to send them freely, and put them down in the petty cash books. The heat here, even now, is awful, and although seated at the table without movement, I am wet through. But the wind is howling, and the dust flying, and so I think we are going to have a storm. It will be a great relief if it does come. With regard to letters, I have told one or two people to write and put "to be forwarded", so these send on please. Others of course you use your discretion about. Those that look like private friends, forward. [...]

Auntie's illness at Dover has knocked all my holiday plans on the head. Poor thing, she is most unlucky. This last year has been a wretched one for her. Mr. Herring wired me yesterday from Dover, that she had been very ill, but was getting better – couldn't move for some days yet. It is congestion of the mucus membrane.

Your illness I suppose was another carbuncle. It seems to me that you always get ill after you have been sailing. [...]

No more today. God bless you. I hope you will soon be able to write yourself and tell me you are all right again.

yr. affec. uncle
A.

Hotelgesellschaft, Thusis A.B.
Viamala
Friday morning

Dear Bertie

Your letter from the "hospital" just arrived, and I am indeed glad to know you have escaped from such terrible trouble as you might have had. Do try now & live <u>regularly</u> – as plainly as you like, but not a feast one day and a fast the next.

I only wish I had attended more to my eating and drinking when I was young – what trouble, pain, and worry I should have avoided.

I sent a telegram home yesterday because I had just received a telegram from Dover saying Auntie had had a relapse, was in bed again, and thought the journey impossible and must give it up. It is no fun for me to stay on alone here, and so I determined to come home. This morning early comes another wire (sent last night I suppose) saying slightly better & still hopes to come abroad. So I shall stay a day or two longer here, until something is definitely decided.

Please tell Clotilde this. If you go to the seaside, why not go to Dover. It is just as dull there as at any other place, & you can look at the steamers going and coming, & it would be a comfort to Auntie to know there was a friend in the same town with her. She wouldn't bother you because all she thinks of is trying to get well. I must stop as the post goes out in five minutes time. I will attend to business matters in another letter.

yr. affect. uncle
A.

Try as we might, we have not been able to discover what Bertie's illness specifically was. Sullivan finds a charming solution as to how he, Clotilde, "Auntie," Bertie, and Louis can all take care of one another.

Hotelgesellschaft, Thusis A.G.
Viamala 10 Aug: 1898
(4.30 London time)

Dear Bertie,

I was just going out for a walk after a wearisome bout of letter writing, when your telegram arrived (10 minutes ago) saying you were well again. I needn't tell you my dear boy what a relief it is to me. For owing to delays somewhere (perhaps on the writers' part) I received no letters until midday today, and have been in a state of suspense since Sunday. I wrote you from Innsbruck on Monday – Clotilde also – so I hope you have the letter by this time. I only learned today from Clotilde's letter what had been the matter with you. How much you must have suffered. Ask Clotilde to read you that of my letter written today, which refers to you, and do, my dear Bertie, take it to heart. Don't grow up into a livery, jaundiced, probably querulous old man. I am not going to write an epistle now, as I want to get out, but I wanted to let you know that I am much relieved. [...]

I shall stay here until I know what Auntie means to do. You didn't know, of course, how ill she has been again. It seems her bad luck always to be ill when alone in a hotel. If she gets strong enough soon, she will come over here and get a little mountain air. The real thing to do, would be for you to bring her over and take care of her, and Clotilde to come with you and take care of you; and then I will take care of Clotilde, and Louis look after the lot of us! That seems to me to be fair all round. It also seems to me that I shan't get out today if I don't stop.

God bless you. Do take better care of yourself and your health. [...]

Your Affectionate uncle A.

Epilogue

"The saddest news..."

In September of 1900, Sullivan caught a chill during another extended trip to Europe. He came home immediately, unknowingly having only ten weeks to live. Bertie was at Sullivan's bedside when Sullivan died. His grief at his uncle's death on November 22nd is described in a letter to his sister Amy (The letter was written on November 22, 1900, meaningfully St. Cecelia's Day, the patron saint of music).

"The saddest news I've ever sent I had to send to you today. It has all been so sudden and rapid and only 12 hours ago he died in my arms. And I loved him so. He was all I had near me to love and now everything is blotted out entirely. What a good, generous soul his was. And we were so united in all our doings. When I wrote you about a fortnight ago, I thought he was really mending. I read him your letter even, so improved was he, but he was so terribly weak and could not fight against the bronchitis which caused the end. I will write more tomorrow, but I am not equal to it now"

Ever the caretaker, Sullivan's will bequeathed sizable sums to each of his nieces and nephews. Bertie received not only the bulk of Sullivan's domestic property, but also those musical scores not otherwise disposed of, and the composer's diaries and other papers. We, the editors, are both distant recipients of his love and generosity.

Musical commemorations followed, most notably a performance at Crystal Palace with selections from Sullivan's *Festival Te Deum,* the *In Memoriam* overture, and the incidental music from *The Tempest* and *Merchant of Venice,* among others.

A memorial was erected, and Gilbert chose a quatrain from *The Yeomen of the Guard:*

Is life a boon?
If so, it must befall
That Death, whene'er he call
Must call too soon.

It is our sincere hope that this collection of letters from Sullivan himself expands the reader's awareness of Sullivan as a person, and reveals at least a little of the humor, warmth, and deep abiding love that he held for his family.

Acknowledgements

We wish to thank the Pierpont Morgan Library in New York City for giving us access to their fine Gilbert and Sullivan collection. We are also grateful to librarians Inge Dupont, Maria Molestina, Sylvie Merian, Vanessa Pintado, and to former Curator of Manuscripts and Books, J. Rigbie Turner, for the thoughtful and professional help given us in gaining access, over the years, to the letters of Sir Arthur Sullivan, his family and others.

We are very grateful to the Sir Arthur Sullivan Society in England for the Society's publication of this book, and for the Society's encouragement of the gathering of these letters from the very beginning. We are particularly grateful to Martin Yates (Chairman of the Sir Arthur Sullivan Society) not only for his strong encouragement, but also for his assistance in the coordination with the printer, development of the books cover, and consistent belief in the books goals.

We want to acknowledge the late Arthur Jacobs for his fine biography of Sullivan. His book has proven much more than helpful in obtaining definitions of so many terms, names and locations. Thanks to John Wolfson for sharing letters from his collection that Sullivan wrote to his (Sullivan's) family.

Thank you to Chris O'Brien for his help in proof reading the script and making helpful editorial suggestions.

We are deeply and particularly grateful to Robin Gordon-Powell for playing a major role in creating the version you are reading. Not only did he make editorial suggestions, he also made scores of formatting suggestions to improve the reading experience. To this end, he even supervised the compilation of the final draft for the printer.

Finally, thanks to Kitty Hayes, for her technical support, encouragement and patience.

Biographical Listing

"Anglesey" – Henry William George Paget, the third Marquess of Anglesey.

Barnett, John Francis – in these letters, this is usually the nephew of the composer of the same name, a Royal Academy colleague of Sullivan, who also studied in Leipzig.

Bendall, Wilfred – secretary to Sullivan, after Walter Smythe.

Benedict, Julius – composer and conductor.

Bennett, William Sterndale – Composer and organist for St. Paul's Cathedral. Sullivan's piano instructor at the Royal Academy of Music

Bridgeman, Christopher – Sullivan's student colleague at the Royal Academy of Music.

Broadwood, Henry – piano manufacturer. He provided scholarship funds for Sullivan, and employed Thomas Sullivan to oversee a band made up of his factory workers.

Cellier, Alfred – musical director for the Opera Comique and a close friend of Sullivan.

Cellier, François – succeeded his brother Alfred as musical director for the Opera Comique and a close friend of Sullivan.

Chorley, Henry Fothergill – noted music critic and Sullivan collaborator.

Clay, Fredric – composer and one of Sullivan's closest friends.

"Clotilde" – housekeeper to Sullivan.

David, Ferdinand – Sullivan's instructor in both conducting and violin at the Leipzig Conservatory.

Davison, James W. – music critic and friend to Sullivan. Occasionally called "Old Jimmy."

Dicey, Edward – editor of The Observer. He became one of Sullivan's closest friends and companions.

Dremel, Mrs. August – close friend of Sullivan's mother, Mary Clementina Sullivan.

Dremel, Sydney – son to Mrs. August Dremel.

Goss, John – Sullivan's professor of harmony at the Royal Academy of Music.

Grant, David Beach – Mr. Grant and his wife were long-time American friends of Sullivan.

Grant, Douglas – son of David Beach Grant.

Grant, Suydam – David Beach Grant's brother.

Grove, George – first director of the Royal College of Music, and the founder and editor of the Dictionary of Music and Musicians. When Grove first encountered Sullivan, he was employed as the administrator for the Crystal Palace.

"Helen" – probably refers to a cousin staying with Sullivan's parents.

Helmore, Thomas – Master of the Children of the Chapel Royal.

Hutchinson, Benjamin – husband to Charlotte Sullivan after Frederic's death.

"Joseph" – servant to Sullivan.

Kistner, Carl Friedrich – music publisher.

Klingemann, Carl – secretary for the Royal Academy of Music's Mendelssohn Scholarship committee.

Lacy, Maud ("Cissie") Helen Sullivan – niece of Sullivan, daughter of Frederic and Charlotte. Married Richard Lacy, son of William Lacy.

Lacy, William – Charlotte's brother.

Lewis, George – Sullivan's friend and legal advisor.

Lindsay, Coutts – Sir Coutts and his wife, Lady Lindsay were long-time friends of Sullivan.

"Louis" – Sullivan's servant.

"Minnie" – a maid for Sullivan.

Montigny-Rémaury, Caroline – a pianist, and Ambroise Thomas' sister-in-law.

Moscheles, Ignaz – pianist, composer, and conductor, and Sullivan's chief piano instructor at the Royal Academy of Music.

Paget, Henry William George – the third Marquess of Anglesey.

Plees, William Gordon – headmaster of a London boarding school attended by Sullivan.

Ronalds, Mary Frances ("Fanny") – American singer and long-time romantic interest of Sullivan. Sometimes called "Auntie" in the letters.

Santley, George – baritone, featured frequently by Sullivan.

Scott Russell, John – patriarch of the Scott Russell family. Sullivan had important relationships with many members of the family, including romances with Russell's daughters Rachel and Louise.

Scott Russell, Louise – third daughter of John Scott Russell.

Scott Russell, Rachel – second daughter of John Scott Russell.

"Silva" – a French servant of Sullivan, initially called "Sylvain".

Smart, George – joint organist and composer for the Chapel Royal.

Smythe, Walter – Sullivan's long-time secretary.

Stephens, Amy (Sullivan) – niece of Sullivan, daughter of Frederic and Charlotte. Also married Charles M. Stephens.

Stephens, Charles – husband to both Florence and Amy Sullivan.

Stephens, Florence (Sullivan) – niece of Sullivan, daughter of Frederic and Charlotte. Married Charles M. Stephens.

Sullivan, Charlotte Louisa Lacy – wife of Frederic Sullivan. Four years after Frederic's death, she married Benjamin Hutchinson.

Sullivan, Frederic – Sullivan's brother. Sometimes called "Fred" or "Jack."

Sullivan, George – nephew of Sullivan.

Sullivan, Herbert ("Bertie") – nephew of Sullivan. After his mother moved to Los Angeles, Bertie lived with Sullivan as his son, though never formally adopted.

Sullivan, Jane ("Janie") – John Sullivan's daughter, Arthur Sullivan's first cousin.

Sullivan, John – Thomas Sullivan's brother, Arthur Sullivan's uncle.

Sullivan, Mary Clementina – Sullivan's mother.

Sullivan, Richard ("Dickie") Frederic – nephew of Sullivan.

Sullivan, Thomas –Arthur Sullivan's father.

Sullivan, William – nephew of Sullivan.

Thomas, Ambroise – the French composer.

Thompson, Henry – surgeon who was a specialist in the treatment of kidney stones.

Bibliography

Books and Journals

Ainger, Michael. *Gilbert and Sullivan: A Dual Biography*. Oxford: New York, 2002. Print.

Apel, Willi, and Ralph T. Daniel. *The Harvard Brief Dictionary of Music*. Cambridge: Harvard UP, 1960. Print.

Baily, Leslie. *The Gilbert and Sullivan Book.* London: Spring, 1966. Print.

Bradley, Ian. *Lost Chords and Christian Soldiers.* London: scm press. 2013. Print.

Cokayne, George E., and Vicary Gibbs. *The Complete Peerage of England, Scotland, Ireland, Great Britain and the United Kingdom: Extant, Extinct or Dormant.* Vol. 1. Gloucester: Sutton, 1984. 140. Print.

Foster, Myles Birket. *The History of the Philharmonic Society of London, 1813-1912*. London: The Bodley Head, 1912. Print.

Hayes, Scott. *Uncle Arthur: The California Connection*. 2nd ed. Sir Arthur Sullivan Society, 2008. Print.

Illing, Robert. *A Dictionary of Music.* Harmondsworth, Middlesex: Penguin, 1950. Print.

Inwood, Stephen. *City of Cities: The Birth of Modern London.* London: Macmillan, 2005. Print.

Jacobs, Arthur. *Arthur Sullivan: A Victorian Musician*. Aldershot: Scolar, 1992. Print.

Lawrence, Arthur. *Sir Arthur Sullivan: Life Story, Letters, and Reminiscences*. Chicago: H.S. Stone, 1900. Print.

Sullivan, Arthur, *Diaries*. Beinecke Rare Book & Manuscript Library, Yale University, New Haven, Conn.

Sullivan, Arthur, *Manuscript letters and manuscripts (various).* Gilbert & Sullivan Collection, Pierpont Morgan Library, New York

Sullivan, Herbert, and Newman Flower. *Sir Arthur Sullivan: His Life, Letters and Diaries*. London: Cassel and, 1950. Print.

Sutton, Elizabeth Madary. *Our Lacy Tree*. Published privately, 2003. Print.

Young, Percy M. *Sir Arthur Sullivan*. New York: W. W. Norton, 1972. Print.

Zeepvat, Charlotte. "Royal Photographers, Sergei Levitsky." *Royal Digest*. 90th ed. Vol. 14. 159. Print.

Websites

Sands, John. "Sullivan and the Covent Garden Promenade Concerts." *The Gilbert and Sullivan Archive*. 6 Aug. 2011. Web. 27 Dec. 2012.

Editor Biographies

W. Scott Hayes, great grandnephew of Arthur Sullivan, received a B.A. in history from U.C. Berkeley. Following two required years in the army, he earned an additional degree in choral music and a secondary teaching credential from San Francisco State University. After teaching both high school history and choral music for a few years more, W. Scott earned a master's degree in counselling, and spent most of the rest of his career in education as a high school counsellor. He retired in 1993. W. Scott has spent much of his retirement researching Sir Arthur Sullivan's relationship to W. Scott's extended family. His book, *Arthur Sullivan: The California Connection*, based on lectures first presented at the Sir Arthur Sullivan Festival at Oxford University in 1996 and the International Gilbert and Sullivan Festival in Berkeley in 1997, was published by the Sir Arthur Sullivan Society in 2001 with a second edition in 2009. He has given lectures at the New York Gilbert and Sullivan Players and Guild, the Lamplighters in San Francisco, San Francisco State University, additional Sullivan Festivals in Cirencester, England, the San Francisco Alumni Chapter of Mu Phi Epsilon (International music fraternity), the Manchester, England Gilbert and Sullivan Society, the London Gilbert and Sullivan Society, Gilbert and Sullivan Society of Victoria, Austin Gilbert and Sullivan Society and the International Gilbert and Sullivan Festival in Buxton, England. He lives with his wife, Kitty, in Petaluma, California.

Scott M. Hayes, great great grandnephew of Arthur Sullivan, is the son of W. Scott Hayes, and currently serves as the associate dean for the School of Communication & Creative Arts at Liberty University. He is an associate professor specializing in acting and directing. He has worked at six universities in the United States and England, and has served as artistic director for two professional companies. He maintains his professional work as a director, actor, and playwright. He is a member of the Screen Actors Guild/American Federation of Television and Radio Artists and Actors Equity Association. His short play *Without Excuse* is published by *Christianity and Theatre*, and his landmark production of *As You Like It* was profiled in *Southern Theatre* magazine. His adaptation of the best-selling novel *Redeeming Love* has been produced all across the United States. Scott served as the editor for the second edition of *Arthur Sullivan: The California Connection*, and is very pleased to have additional opportunities to work closely with his father. He lives with his wife, Sarah, and three daughters in Forest, Virginia.